The Saga of
LUCY MCGREGOR

Johnnie G. Love

Johnnie G. Love
Hope you Enjoy !

This book is a work of fiction. Names, characters, places and incidents are either products of the author's imagination or are used fictitiously. Any resemblance to actual events, locales or persons, living or dead, is entirely coincidental.

ISBN: 1456364227
ISBN-13: 9781456364229

This book is dedicated to the memory of my mother,
Lucille Sides Gadd, who has been an inspiration to
me every day of my life.

The Saga of
Lucy McGregor

A Story of Courage and Survival

Johnnie G. Love

PROLOGUE

Something had awakened Lucy from a sound sleep. She lay listening for a moment and realized it was her little dog, Tiger. He was whining softly outside the bedroom window. Tiger had shown up at Lucy's house one day and lay trembling on the ground as she approached. Lucy saw in the dog something of herself. She fed and petted him until the shivering of his little body ceased. He had been Lucy's dog from that moment. Lucy got out of bed and made her way to the window. A full moon cast an eerie light over the landscape of the yard. A movement caught her eye near the small rose bush she had planted a few days before. She squinted her eyes and realized the thing moving about on the ground was her husband of forty two years, Junior.

Junior had left the house late that afternoon without a word to Lucy. She knew he would be heading to the nearby "beer joint," as the locals called it. It was no more than a shack, hidden back in the woods off the main road. Lucy knew a lot of questionable activities went on there but did not care that Junior chose to spend his time there. It took him out of the house and away from her.

Lucy rose and went to the front of the house where she could get a better view. She could hear Junior's voice now but could not make out the garbled sounds. She was sure he was trying to call out to her but made no move in his direction.

Junior had been having dizzy spells lately and had finally gone to the county nurse. He was told he had dangerously high blood pressure and was given a prescription for medication. Junior just tossed it away. "He had better things to spend his money on," he had told Lucy. He was thrashing about wildly now, but still, Lucy could not move. She knew the thing he had been warned about had happened. The nurse had told Junior he could have a stroke if he failed to take his medication.

Lucy knew she should do the humane thing and help him but she could not make herself move. She pulled up her rocker and sat in front of the window, watching her husband as if in a trance. All the years of neglect, abuse and torture held her in that chair.
She sat there in the dim moonlight and thought back to when it all started, so many years before.

Lucy – The Beginning

CHAPTER I

Lucy was awakened in the early hours just before dawn by the sound of cries from her mother. She was only nine but she knew something was terribly wrong. She lay wide awake now and listened to the muffled sounds coming from the next room. Her two younger sisters lay in the bed next to her but remained asleep, for which Lucy was grateful. Her mother had not been well for the past few months and the care of the younger children had fallen on Lucy's small shoulders. It was awfully cold in the room where she and her sisters slept. She snuggled deeper under the covers and covered her ears in an attempt to block out the awful sounds.

The log cabin consisted of two rooms, the one in which Lucy now slept and the larger room which served as the kitchen and bedroom for her parents. There was a large fireplace over which their meals were prepared. Lucy was unsure what she should do. It was nearing dawn and normally she would have been up fetching water and helping her mother prepare the morning meal. Today, however, she instinctively knew she should stay where she was until her mother's cries could no longer be heard.

The day before, Lucy's grandmother had arrived to help with the "birthing" as Granny Alva had called it. She had brought with her peppermint sticks for Lucy and the two younger children. They loved Granny Alva, not because of the candy, although that did not hurt, but she always told them the most wonderful stories of when she was a little girl.

Lucy could only hear the sound of her Granny now and what sounded like sobs coming from her father. But that couldn't be, thought Lucy, as she had never seen her father cry. Unable to lie in bed any longer, Lucy pulled back the quilts and moved as quietly as possible to the doorway which separated the rooms.

She could see her father through the crack in the door, his head in his hands and Granny Alva trying to comfort him. Lucy ran through the door but stopped short as she saw her mother lying lifeless on the bed with what appeared to be a small bundle of bloody towels at her side. Lucy began to back away with a whimper so low it could hardly be heard. Granny Alva looked up and pulled Lucy into her arms. In her softest voice, she tried to explain to Lucy that her mother was now in heaven and so was their baby brother. She explained to Lucy that her mother had not been well and was not strong enough to survive the birth. The baby had died as well. Lucy's father raised his head and with a look that Lucy hoped she would never see again, walked slowly out the front door.

Granny Alva explained to Lucy there would have to be a burial. The family could not afford a fancy funeral so Lucy's father would build a pine box that would hold the body of her mother as well as the baby. They would be buried in the old cemetery behind the small church Granny Alva attended.

Lucy knew without question that all the responsibilities of the house would now be hers. Her sisters, Greta, only three years of age and Marcy, only five, would now be totally dependent on her for all their care. Lucy's father was a farmer and hunter and knew nothing of housework or cooking.

Lucy had attended the small school nearby for three years. She could now read on the most basic level and knew a little math, but returning to school would be out of the question. She accepted her fate with little complaint. Her outlook on life then, and the hard years to come was to accept your fate and do what you must to survive.

CHAPTER 2

The years slipped by with little change for Lucy. The cabin had been improved with a wood burning stove for the cooking. This made Lucy's life of drudgery a little easier. Her days were filled with the chores of daily living. There was always the worry of having enough food to eat.

Since her mother's death, her father had shown little interest in the daily activities of the house. He would be gone sometimes for days and Lucy would start to panic as the small food supply would begin to dwindle. He would always show up though, bringing with him a turkey or some other small game. There was usually a bag of cornmeal and flour for which Lucy was grateful. She could always make corn bread and biscuits to fill their stomachs if the other food ran out. The flour and corn meal came in printed cloth bags which Lucy used to make clothing for her self and the girls.

Lucy managed to plant a small garden in the back of the house each year which supplied them with vegetables throughout the summer months. She preserved what wasn't eaten, using the canning jars Granny Alva

had given her. There were wild black berries picked
and canned. Potatoes, dried beans, walnuts and chest-
nuts were also a food staple to carry them through the
winter. There was never an end to the work involved
in just surviving. There were no luxuries whatsoever.
Lucy made their soap in the manner her mother had
taught her. This was used for bathing, laundry and
dishwashing. Their water was fetched from a natural spring nearby. Water for laundry and bathing was
captured in a rain barrel placed under a drain pipe
from the roof of the house. With no indoor plumb-
ing, a trip to the outhouse on cold winter mornings
was nothing to look forward to.

Little Greta and Marcy had thrived and appeared to
be doing well under the circumstances. Lucy was
proud of the job she had done and felt a sense of accomplishment. She had done well with the hand life
had dealt her. The girls were older now and Lucy began to dream of a life of her own. Little Greta was now
nine years of age and Marcy eleven. Lucy had taught
them self reliance and independence. She knew life
was hard and they needed to be prepared for any circumstances coming their way.

Through out the years, Lucy and the girls occasionally attended church with their Granny Alva. Lucy always looked forward to these Sunday outings as it was
her only social outlet. She had no friends and had
little contact with the other young people in the community. She knew most by name as that is the way in
small country communities but there were no picnics
or social events for Lucy. On occasion she had heard

the whispers about their clothes and shoes and the fact that Lucy did not attend school. This hurt Lucy deeply but she held her head high. The one thing she had that no one could take away was her pride. It was the one thing that sustained her as well as her dreams of one day having a life and family of her own.

Granny Alva had come by the day before, bringing her usual peppermint sticks and a few other things she thought the girls might need. Granny lived on the route of the "Rolling Store" as all the local residents called it. Mr. Tom Johnson had come up with the idea. Most of the rural residents did not own automobiles and getting to the local store was a real hardship. Mr. Johnson had built a covering over the back of a flat bed truck and filled it with food staples such as dried beans, flour, sugar, cornmeal and lard. Of course there were a few items which could be considered luxury items in those days, such as soap, shampoo and talcum powder. He also carried a good supply of pots, pans, wash tubs and rub boards.

Before leaving, Granny Alva asked Lucy if she and the girls would come to church services the next day. She explained they were having "home coming." This was usually a big event as the church was the hub of all social activities and most of the local residents would attend, even what some considered the worst of sinners. As was the custom of such events, the women who attended would bring enough food to feed their own families plus a little extra for the less fortunate.

Knowing Lucy's circumstances and her fierce pride, Granny Alva explained tactfully that she had fried too much chicken the day before so it would not be necessary for Lucy and the girls to bring food.

When Granny Alva left, Lucy and the girls sprang into action, more excited than they had been in days. They had one good dress each that was saved for such occasions. Granny Alva had ordered them from the Sears & Roebuck catalog the month before. Lucy had never had a store bought dress and she thought it was the most beautiful thing she had ever seen. She kept the dresses hanging on a nail driven into the wall as there were no closets in the cabin. No one was allowed to touch those dresses unless it was for such an occasion as this.

Granny Alva had also ordered them each a pair of shoes. The shoes were all a little too big so Lucy stuffed paper into the toes to keep them on their feet and make them a little more comfortable. Lucy suspected that Granny Alva had ordered them a size too large knowing they would out grow them before they got much use of them. Shoes were a luxury and were not worn at all in the summer months unless you were going to church or some other special occasion.

Sunday morning came and Lucy was up earlier than usual. She wanted to wash her hair before she had to prepare the morning meal. On days such as this, Lucy would think of her mother and whish she could be here. She remembered seeing her mother use eggs to wash her hair when she wanted it to look especially nice. Lucy had thought it an odd thing to do but had found it worked quite well in the absence of shampoo. The egg whites made a great lather and the hair was silky and shiny afterwards.

Lucy had long black hair she had inherited from her great grandmother who was a full blooded Cherokee. It had a natural wave and was very beautiful when she wore it hanging down her back. She never gave much thought to her looks. Most of her days were spent in and around their cabin going about her chores. She had little contact with the outside world, other than Granny Alva.

As Lucy grew older and her body began to change into that of a young woman, she was quite unaware of just how beautiful she was. Recently, she had begun to notice the boys at Granny Alva's church. They would grin at her and she would catch them poking each other and laughing at some unknown joke. Lucy suspected it had something to do with her.

She noticed one boy in particular, the preacher's son. He was not unusually handsome but there was something about him that brought a warm flush to her cheeks each time she caught him sneaking a peek at her. She hoped he would be there this Sunday and that she might be able to muster up the courage to speak to him.

The church was about two miles from the cabin but Lucy and the girls did not mind the walk at all today. It was a beautiful summer day and they were all excited as they made their way down the dirt road to the church. Granny Alva was to meet them there. She lived about a mile from the church in the opposite direction from where Lucy lived and Uncle Thomas was to carry her, along with the food in his wagon. Wagons were the common mode of transportation for most of the farmers in the area. A few people had horses, even a few had an old truck, but most all had mules and wagons which were used primarily for farm work.

The girls weren't the only ones walking to church today. As they made their way down the road, they caught up with others who weren't quite so eager to get there. One of them was Junior, Reverend John McGregor's son, and her heart beat a little faster. He had been named after his father but everyone called him Junior to avoid confusing the two. She noticed he began to lag behind his friends and walked slower until Lucy and the girls caught up to him.

"I know you" he said with a cocky grin. "You're that girl, Lucy that lives over in Chicken Holler."

"Yes," Lucy replied, "and you are Junior, Preacher John's son."

"Yep," said Junior, falling into step beside Lucy, "and you know preacher's boys are always good boys."

Lucy did not know what to say to that comment. Greta and Marcy noticed how nervous Lucy was and began to giggle. They skipped on ahead of Lucy and Junior, whispering and giggling as they went. Lucy could feel her cheeks turning red as she walked along beside Junior, casting a glance his way every now and then.

"Would you like to come eat with us after church services?" asked Junior.

"I don't know, I have to talk to Granny Alva first," Lucy replied.

As they came within sight of the church, Junior ran on ahead of Lucy, turning to grin at her as he went. He knew the other boys would be teasing him when he caught up to them and did not want Lucy to hear. Of course Lucy did not know of his boasts earlier of how he was going to "get that Lucy and kiss her out behind the church."

All the boys thought Lucy was one of the prettiest girls around but were afraid to approach her as she never seemed interested in any of them. There were whispers about her not attending school and how she had to take care of her sisters as if they were her own. Junior had heard comments from his father about Lucy's "no account daddy" and knew life must be very hard for Lucy and her sisters. If his disposition were different, he might have felt sorry for her, but Junior was a little spoiled and thought only of himself. He had made up his mind he wanted Lucy and he was going to have her.

Granny Alva was already there when Lucy and her sisters arrived at the church. Tables of a crude

fashion had been set up in various areas across the
church grounds. Some would use the bed of their
wagons and others would simply spread a blanket
under the many old oak trees which surrounded the
church.

Lucy was hesitant to ask Granny Alva about her invitation to eat lunch with the Reverend and his family.
She did not know how she would react as Lucy had
never shown any interest in boys before. To Lucy's
surprise, however, Granny Alva thought it would be a
wonderful idea. The Reverend had a large family so
Lucy would be well chaperoned.   Truthfully, Granny
Alva was pleased that Lucy had the opportunity to
spend a little time with children of her own age. She
hoped that Lucy would be able to find a nice young
man someday and have a home of her own. Lord
knew she deserved it.

After the rousing church service, everyone spilled out
the church doors eager to get about the business of
eating and socializing. Lucy wasn't sure just what she
should do about her invitation. She stood with her
own family in indecision. Junior appeared out of the
crowd and headed straight for Lucy.

"Howdy, Ms. Alva, I've come to ask your permission
for Lucy to eat with us today."

Granny Alva was impressed and pleased that Junior
would have the manners to ask her permission. Little
did she know, however, Junior was a sly one and did
not have the best intentions for Lucy.

Reverend John and Ms. Allie, as everyone called the Reverend's wife, were already seated in cane bottom chairs. A plate of food was being served to them by their eldest daughter. The blessing had been said at the end of the church service as Reverend John knew it would be hard to get everyone together afterwards. Lucy was so nervous it was all she could do to keep her hands from trembling so she kept them clutched by her side.

"Hello, Ms. Allie, Reverend John," Lucy mumbled, as Junior motioned for her to take a seat on the blanket spread at the Reverend's feet. Junior had five sisters and two older brothers. Junior was the youngest boy with only one sister younger than himself. Everyone seemed to dote on Junior and he certainly knew how to get what he wanted.

Lucy ate in silence listening to the chatter and laughter around her. She was totally aware of Junior sitting next to her as his arm would brush hers every few seconds. Lucy suspected it was intentional but deep down she kind of enjoyed the thrill that went through her each time it happened. These feelings were totally foreign to her as she had led such a sheltered life.

Everyone seemed to ignore Lucy for the most part, which was fine with her. She was enjoying listening to the kidding and joking among the siblings. When everyone had finished eating, Lucy offered to help pack up the few leftovers and clean up. Junior had other ideas, however, and grabbed Lucy by the hand, pulling her to her feet.

"We are going for a little walk," he announced, without consulting with Lucy. Not knowing how to get out of the situation, Lucy went along, looking across the grounds for her grandmother.

"Don't worry about Ms. Alva," Junior stated. "She won't mind if we take a little walk."

Lucy had caught her grandmother's eye and saw no signs of disapproval so she let Junior lead her across the grounds toward the old cemetery.

Lucy visited her mother's grave each time she came to church, removing any grass or twigs which may be littering the grave. Oh, how she wished her mother was here now to give her advice. She loved Granny Alva dearly but she would not dream of discussing boys and such with her. It terrified Lucy to think about getting married and having children after what happened to her mother but at the same time, she wanted a family of her own.

Lucy and Junior strolled among the grave sites with Junior pointing out where various relatives were buried. It seemed half the cemetery held some member of his family.

Lucy did not notice they had worked their way around behind the church and were no longer in view of Granny Alva and the others. She did notice, however, when Junior grabbed her hand and pulled her closer to him. This startled Lucy but at the same time she rather enjoyed it and did not pull away. Noting little resistance from Lucy, Junior took this as a sign of permission to go forward. He pulled Lucy behind a big oak tree and before Lucy knew what was happening, kissed her hard on the mouth.

Lucy was upset that he would be so forward with her but at the same time she did not want to make him angry. She could not help but feel a shiver when he kissed her even though it was not what she had expected or dreamed about. She had imagined a gentle soft embrace and a slow, passionate kiss. This was neither. Junior was rough and had actually bruised her lips a little. Not having any experience in these matters, Lucy thought maybe this was normal and all kisses were this way.

Junior seemed to be pleased with his accomplishment and was eager to get back to his friends to brag about it. "I had better get you back to Ms. Alva before she comes looking for us," he told Lucy.

Confused, Lucy followed him back to the crowd of people who were now starting to pack up and head home. When they got back to Uncle Thomas's wagon, Junior rushed away throwing a "see you" over his shoulder as he went.

Lucy had little to say on the long walk back home. She was confused and near tears. Little Greta and Marcy seemed not to notice as they chatted excitedly about the day's events. Lucy did not know if Junior was really interested in her or if he had just wanted to kiss her. Although she really did not give him permission, she could have done more to stop it, had she been more experienced in such matters.

Days went by with the same drudgery for Lucy. She would catch herself thinking about Junior and that kiss. Maybe it wasn't like she remembered at all. She would close her eyes and imagine she could feel Junior's lips pressing softly to hers. Maybe in the excitement of the moment it had only felt like Junior was being a bit rough. There was no one she could talk to, no girlfriends to confide in or ask for advice.

One day, out of the blue, Junior showed up at Lucy's front door. Lucy's father was off on one of his trips, so Lucy and the girls were home alone. Granny Alva was about the only visitor Lucy ever had so she was startled to see Junior standing there when she opened the door.

"Hey, was in the area hunting so thought I would stop by and say hi," said Junior.

Not wanting Junior to see how poorly they lived, Lucy stepped outside and closed the door. "Would you like to sit down?" Lucy asked, indicating the steps leading into the cabin.

"Why sure, don't mind if I do," stated Junior and sat down as close to Lucy as he could get. "I've been thinking about you and that kiss since I saw you last," he said.

Lucy did not know what to say, so she just sat there and waited.

"How would you like to come to my house for dinner this Sunday after church?" asked Junior.

"That would be nice," answered Lucy, "if it is alright with Ms. Allie."

"Oh she won't mind. One more mouth won't make much difference," said Junior. "You can ride home with us after church, if you would like to go."

"All right, if you are sure Ms. Allie won't mind," answered Lucy.

"Good, see you then," Junior called, as he picked up his old shotgun and strolled away, turning to give Lucy a wink.

Lucy had two days to think about and prepare for her Sunday date. She hated to wear the same dress as Junior had already seen her in it but she had no choice. Maybe she could do something different with her hair, she thought. Noticing the wild roses growing in the edge of the woods, she decided it might be nice to pin some in her hair. They were pink like her dress and might look pretty in her black hair. They also smelled quite nice.

She worried that she did not have the proper under garments but knew no one would know but her. She had made panties for herself and the girls from the white bags their flour came in and used old inner-tube rubber for the elastic. She did not have a bra but really had no need for one as her body was young and firm. A lot of the young girls of her time did not have such undergarments.

Having no modern toiletries, Lucy would cut twigs from a tree branch and chew the end until it was soft. This was used along with baking soda to clean their teeth. Lucy thought about all these things as she went about readying herself for her date. It was amazing they could survive on so little, she thought.

Sunday morning, Lucy explained to Greta and Marcy, she would not be walking home with them that afternoon. When Lucy told them she had been invited by Junior to have lunch at the Reverend's house, the girls were unmerciful in their teasing.

They loved Lucy dearly as she was like a mother to them. They were happy she was having some time to herself for a change. At the same time, they worried about the time she might get married and leave them. When these fears began to bother them, they reminded themselves that Lucy had been younger than they when their mother had died. She had sacrificed everything to take care of them.

This was the first Sunday Lucy had attended church since Home Coming. As she and the girls walked into the church and took their seats next to Granny Alva, Lucy nervously looked around for Junior. She caught his eye as he sat down on the back row with some of his friends and he gave her a wink.

Lucy noticed the boys poking each other and laughing. She wondered what the big joke was. She would have died had she known it was her they were laughing about. Of course she did not know Junior had bragged about their kiss and embellished the telling of it to all his friends. She felt her cheeks turning red and turned her attention to Reverend John and the fire and brim-stone sermon he was preaching.

When the church services were over, Lucy explained to Granny Alva that she had been invited to lunch with Junior and his family. Granny Alva told her that was a wonderful idea and cautioned Lucy to stay with the family and not wander away with Junior. She told her to make Junior bring her straight home after they were through with lunch.

Granny Alva had discretely done some checking on Junior and had heard some things she did not like. However, she did not want to spoil this for Lucy if it was what she wanted.

Lucy and the Reverend's family all loaded into the wagon and headed home. Lucy had passed their house on occasion and thought it quite impressive. However, she had little to compare it to. She only knew it was much larger and nicer than their little cabin. She had never been inside but thought the white paint and front porch that ran along the entire front of the house was lovely.

Ms. Allie had the most wonderful peonies planted in the yard and Lucy thought they were beautiful. The house was situated on over 200 acres of farm and timber land. Reverend John did little farming, however, the older boys did. As they had married, the Reverend had given them their own little section of land and a small house was built for each. To Lucy, Junior's family was rich.

Upon arriving at the house, they all clambered out of the wagon and rushed inside as everyone was hungry and eager to eat. Lucy felt very awkward and shyly followed the group inside.

She was impressed with the interior of the house as well. They actually had wall paper on the walls and linoleum on the floors. There were fireplaces in the living room as well as the bedrooms. There were huge feather beds which looked like you could totally disappear in them. There was even an ice box in the kitchen which could keep ice for several days. The house only had four large rooms but it seemed huge to Lucy.

Lucy asked Ms. Allie if she could be of any help, but before she could answer, Junior grabbed her by the hand and led her to the swing on the front porch.

Most of the boys in the area wore overalls but today Junior had on slacks and a white shirt with the sleeves rolled up above the elbows. Lucy noticed the muscles on his upper arm and how the tan line stopped at the edge of the rolled up sleeve. She felt a little uncomfortable as Junior moved closer to her and placed his arm across the back of the swing.

"I've been thinking about you a lot," said Junior.

"I've thought about you too," said Lucy shyly.

"I'd really like to spend more time with you," Junior said as he slid his hand down to Lucy's back. "What do you think about that?"

"I think that would be nice," Lucy said, as she sat up from the back of the swing. She hoped that Junior understood she was uncomfortable with him sitting so close to her. He did not seem to notice but leaned in closer, as if to kiss her. Lucy just knew Ms. Allie or even worse, Reverend John, might come out the door at any moment. She would die if she was caught kissing Junior. She sprang up from the swing and backed towards the door.

"We really should be getting inside. I imagine Ms. Allie has lunch ready by now," said Lucy.

"Oh alright," Junior grumbled, "I am starved anyway."

Everyone was seated around a long table which had a chair at each end and a bench on either side. Reverend John sat at the head of the table and Ms. Allie at the other end. All the children were seated on either side of the table crammed together on the benches. Ms. Allie was up more than she was seated, however, refilling the bowls and bread basket as the food disappeared. These people sure have hearty appetites, thought Lucy. The food they consumed in that one meal would have lasted her family a week.

After lunch Lucy helped the girls clear the table and wash the dishes while Ms. Allie relaxed on the front porch. It was not unusual for a neighbor to drop by and sit and chat awhile and today was no exception. Lucy wondered where Junior had gotten off to when he came strolling in the back door.

"If you are about ready, guess I had better get you on back home." Junior said.

Lucy was a little surprised. She had assumed she would stay and visit awhile with Junior's sisters and Ms. Allie before leaving. She thought it rude to just up and leave so soon after eating. She guessed that Junior had something else he wanted to do so said her goodbyes and thanked Ms. Allie for the lunch. She noticed that Junior had his mule in front of the house and wasn't sure what to say when he indicated they would be riding the mule home. Junior grinned, hopped on the mules back and reached down to help Lucy up behind him.

Lucy felt a little uncomfortable sitting astride the mule with her dress hiked up and clinging to Junior's back. Junior brought the mule to a trot and Lucy had to put her arms around him to avoid falling off. She could feel the warmth of his body through the thin material of his shirt and felt a strange stirring within her. She wandered if what she was feeling could be love. She had no way of knowing Junior chose to ride the mule instead of taking the wagon for this very purpose. He knew he could not have this closeness with her if they had taken the wagon.

They were a short distance from Lucy's cabin when Junior stopped the mule and hopped off.

"What's wrong?" asked Lucy.

"Oh, I thought we might take a rest under that old oak tree over there and talk awhile."

Lucy wasn't quite sure what to say but saw no harm in it since it was still early in the day and the girls would not be expecting her home yet.

Junior tied the mule's reign to an over head limb and pulled Lucy down on the soft grass beside him. He knew it was highly unlikely that anyone would be coming along the road this time of the day. Most people were still at home enjoying their Sunday lunch so there was very little traffic along the road.

Junior edged closer to Lucy and put his arm around her shoulder. "Them roses sure smell nice," he said as he leaned in and sniffed her hair.

Lucy had almost forgotten about the roses she had pinned in her hair earlier. She was sure they were wilted by now. "There is a whole bush of them back at our cabin," said Lucy, not quite sure what to say.

"Well they sure look pretty in your hair," said Junior, and pulled her closer to him.

Before she knew what was happening, Junior had pulled her back on the grass and was kissing her hard on the mouth. Lucy began to panic as things seemed to be getting out of hand. She tried to push Junior away which made him even more excited.

"I just want a little kiss," said Junior. "Come on Lucy, you know you like it too."

Lucy felt tears coming to her eyes and prayed she would not start crying. Oh how will I get out of this, she thought, and was on the verge of panic when she heard the faint sound of an engine. Junior must have heard it too because he let go of Lucy and stood, reaching for the mule's reigns. Before he could get himself and Lucy back on the mule, an old truck came slowly around the bend of the road. It was old Mr. Duncan on his way home after having lunch with the widow Lawrence.

To Lucy's surprise, she saw her father in the passenger seat as the truck slowed to a stop. Her father had been gone for two days and was on his way home when he was given a ride by Mr. Duncan.

"What you doing out here, girl?" asked Lucy's Paw.

"I had lunch with the Reverend and Ms. Allie after church, Paw, and Junior was giving me a ride home."

"Well, you're almost home now, so it won't be necessary for Junior to go any further. You can just walk on with me," he said, stepping out of the truck.

Junior did not protest as Lucy's Paw seemed to see right through him. He glanced guiltily at Lucy, mumbled his farewell, and trotted away. Lucy was relieved but at the same time wondered if Junior would ever speak to her again. She felt like such an ignorant fool. How was she supposed to react to all of this? Maybe, if she could muster up the courage, she would speak to Granny Alva about it when she next visited.

"Everything alright at the cabin?" asked Lucy's father.

"Yes Paw," said Lucy, feeling a little ashamed and hoped her father did not notice the flush on her cheeks.

"You're getting older girl and the boys are going to start buzzing around you like bees to honey. I guess I had better stick a little closer to home Lucy. I know I haven't been around the way I should have but that's gonna change. You got your maw's good looks Lucy, and you are a good girl. I don't want to see any harm come to you. You need to be careful with these boys."

"I will Paw," said Lucy, feeling more than a little uncomfortable.

Her father had been like a shadow figure over the years, coming and going with hardly a word. It touched Lucy, that for the first time in years, her father really seemed to care what happened to her.

CHAPTER 3

Junior rode his mule at full gallop back home. He was so mad he could hardly stand it. If that no good Paw of Lucy's had not shown up, he would have had her for sure.

Junior was used to getting what he wanted, and Lucy would be no exception. He had to have her and he was going to find a way. The answer came the very next day when Reverend John called Junior in and told him it was time they had a little talk.

"What about daddy?" asked Junior, a little concerned as this usually meant he was in some kind of trouble.

"I couldn't help but notice you and that little Lucy girl yesterday and I think it is time you settled down."

"You mean get married, daddy?" asked Junior, not sure how he felt about the matter.

"Yes," said Reverend John. "You could do a lot worse than that Lucy. She's a good girl and a hard worker. She's taken care of those sisters of hers since they were babies and she would make a good mother to your children."

"I'll think about it," said Junior, not sure he liked the idea at all as he still had some wild oats to sow.

For the next few days, Junior did exactly that. All day long his thoughts would turn to Lucy. It might be good to have a house of his own and not have his daddy breathing down his neck all the time.

When Junior's older brothers had gotten married his father had given them twenty five acres of land each and a small house was built on that land by the entire family. If he was married to Lucy he could have her when ever he wanted. The more he thought about it the more he liked the idea.

Junior spoke to his father, and it was settled. If he could get Lucy to agree to marry him, the deed would be signed for Junior's twenty five acres and they would start on the house.

Love never entered Junior's mind. He just knew he was attracted to Lucy as he had been to no other girl, and if marrying her was the cost of having her, then marry her he would. He never considered she might say no. After all, look at what all he had to offer, he reasoned. She could do a lot worse. She should be proud that he would even consider marrying her. Why, she didn't even have shoes to wear half the time and that cabin she lived in was hardly habitable.

Junior decided he would approach Ms. Alva after church next Sunday and tell her he would like to marry Lucy. He knew her Paw would probably be

gone by then and he would rather ask Ms. Alva anyway. He would have preferred to go straight to Lucy
but knew that was out of the question. It was expected
of a young man that he get the approval of the girls
father, however, if her Paw wasn't around, Junior felt
it would be appropriate to ask Ms. Alva in his stead.

Sunday morning came and Junior could hardly contain himself as he sat in the back row with the rest
of the boys. All the young men sat as far away from
Reverend John as they could get. Sometimes, they
felt his piercing eyes could see right through to their
souls.

The back of the pew in front of the boys held any
number of initials which had been carved there over
the years, even that of Reverend John when he was a
boy. The church was ninety eight years old and had
quite a history.

Junior looked at Ms. Alva sitting in her usual seat and
was grateful that Lucy was not with her today. As soon
as the church service was over, Junior rushed outside
to wait for Ms. Alva.

He had quite a long wait as Ms. Alva stopped and chatted with everyone on her way out. Junior became more
nervous the longer he waited. He had just about lost
his nerve when he saw Ms. Alva coming his way.

"Afternoon, Ms. Alva," said Junior. "Could I speak to
you for a few minutes if you have the time?"

"Why yes Junior, is there something in particular you wanted to talk to me about?" Ms. Alva asked, as she noticed how nervous Junior seemed.

"Well, as you know, I have taken quite a liking to your Lucy and I would like to ask for her hand in marriage," Junior said as he shifted from one foot to the other.

Ms. Alva was shocked and could not think of a thing to say for the moment. She finally composed herself and said, "Well Junior, have you spoken to Lucy about this?"

"Not yet, but I plan to go over and ask her as soon as I leave here if I have your permission."

Ms. Alva did not feel comfortable giving Junior her approval until she had spoken to Lucy. "Alright Junior, you have my approval and I am sure that of her Paw, if it is what Lucy wants. However, I want you to wait about speaking to her until I have a chance to talk to her."

Junior was impatient and a bit put off. This old biddy should be ecstatic that he would even consider marrying her granddaughter. Never the less, he agreed and left with the promise from Granny Alva that she would speak to Lucy that very afternoon.

Granny Alva had not planned to visit Lucy and the girls today but knew when she explained the situation to Thomas, he would not mind taking her by to see them.

Lucy was surprised to see Granny Alva when she opened the door but was glad to see her. She grew quite lonely at times and since the incident with Junior, she had been hoping to talk to Granny Alva about it.

"How are you Lucy?" asked Granny Alva, as she took a seat on the top step.

Little Greta and Marcy came running out expecting their usual peppermint sticks but were disappointed when Granny Alva explained she had not known she was coming, so therefore, there would be no candy today. Crestfallen, the girls left to return to their game of checkers, which was their favorite pastime.

"Lucy, I have something I need to discuss with you," said Granny Alva.

Lucy's heart beat a little faster as she sank down beside her. Had her father told her about seeing her with Junior?

"That boy, Junior, way laid me after church today and asked me for permission to marry you," said Granny Alva, as she watched Lucy closely. She loved the girl dearly and would rather die than see any harm come to her.

"He what?" stammered Lucy, in shock.

"That's right, he said he is ready to settle down and wants you to be his wife." "How do you feel about that Lucy?" asked Granny Alva.

"Why I don't really know Granny. I have not even thought about that," said Lucy.

Granny Alva could see the confusion and uncertainty on her face. "I want you to think about it carefully Lucy." She was not sure Junior would make a good husband for Lucy. There was something about him that made her uneasy.

"Lucy, you have to make this decision yourself. Just weigh all the good reasons you should marry him against the reasons you feel you shouldn't. He has some good things to offer, such as a home and a plot of land of your own."

She explained to Lucy what Junior had told her of Reverend John's promise of a plot of land and a house.

"Little Greta and Marcy are old enough to take care of themselves now and you deserve some happiness. However, there are things more important than property Lucy, such as love, respect and caring for one another, through thick and thin."

"I know Granny, and I promise I will think abut it carefully before making a decision," Lucy promised.

Uncle Thomas came by and Granny Alva left, leaving behind a bewildered and confused Lucy. A home of her own, she thought. Maybe she could have linoleum on her floors, at least in the kitchen, and even curtains on the windows. Junior frightened her a little and she hardly knew him. Still, there was something about him that excited her. She knew little of relationships between men and women and knew she must talk to Granny Alva whether she wanted to or not.

CHAPTER 4

Lucy's Paw came home that night, exhausted after a day of chopping wood. This was the one thing he always took care of. He always saw that Lucy had a good supply of wood for the cook stove. In the winter, even more was needed for the fireplace. He knew Lucy could handle the rest and had no qualms about leaving his children alone for days at a time. He had never talked to Lucy about their financial situation or where he went on the days he was not home. Maybe it would have made her and the girls feel better had he shared that with them. Truth was, he was out roaming the area picking up odd jobs where ever he could find work. Times were hard and there was not a lot available, still he managed to earn enough to keep the girls supplied with the absolute necessities. He had given up on trying to farm when Lucy's mother had died. All the will and drive had just dried up and left him.

After their evening meal, with Greta and Marcy already in bed, Lucy decided to approach her father about Junior's offer of marriage. There was no sofa or other such modern seating in Lucy's cabin, just four cane bottomed chairs. These served them well around the small table at meal time, but they were not the most comfortable seating for socializing.

She took the chair closest to her father and noticed how old he looked in the dim lamp light. She felt a strange tug at her heart, and remembered how wonderful and loving he had been before her mother had died. This gave her the courage to speak, knowing somewhere inside him there had to be some of that love left.

"Paw, I need to talk to you about something very important," Lucy said timidly.

Lucy's father slowly raised his head and looked at Lucy, not sure he wanted to hear what she had to say.

"Junior asked Granny Alva for my hand in marriage today Paw." Not wanting his feelings to be hurt, Lucy went on. "He told Granny Alva he would have asked you but you were not here."

Lucy's Paw looked at her for a moment, then, took her hand in his. That simple gesture brought tears to Lucy's eyes. She could not remember the last time her father had hugged her or touched her.

"Lucy, I know I haven't been the father I should and I can't make any excuses except that I have provided the best I knew how. After your mother died I felt like a part of me died too. I don't know what I would have done without you all these years, girl. You've grown up without me hardly noticing. I guess the time has come for you to start thinking about a family of your own, but do you think Junior is the right boy for you?" he asked gently.

"I don't really know Paw," Lucy said, feeling a little more comfortable. "I don't know him that well yet, but I am sure he doesn't mean right away. Reverend John has promised to give him some land and build a house for us. I thought we could do our courting while the house is being built."

"Do you have feelings for him Lucy?" asked her father, trying not to embarrass her.

"I am not really sure what I feel Paw. I know I can hardly get my breath when he is around but at the same time he scares me a little."

"Well, I guess that's natural Lucy, as you haven't had any experience with boys. This is such an important step, but I want you to be happy. When you have gotten to know Junior a little better, if you still want to marry him, then you have my blessings."

"Thank you Paw," said Lucy and hugged her father's neck for the first time since she was a little girl.

"I love you girl," said her father with tears in his eyes.

CHAPTER 5

Time seemed to drag for Lucy. It had been three whole days since she had spoken to her father about Junior. There had been no sign of him and Lucy began to think maybe he had changed his mind. Maybe he did not want to marry her after all. She had done nothing but think about the possibility since Granny Alva's visit.

In fact, she had thought about it so much, she had convinced herself of how wonderful it would be. She would marry Junior and have a nice house to live in. She pictured herself cooking his meals, doing his laundry and having him come home to her at night after a day in the fields. She would have him a warm bath ready, they would laugh and eat together and then snuggle up in one of those soft feather beds for the night. He would hold her gently in his arms and kiss her softly on the lips until they fell asleep. This was as far as Lucy would get in her day dreams as she knew nothing of what was expected of a new bride.

On the fourth day, Lucy answered a knock at her door and was surprised but excited to see Junior there. The girls were at school so they were alone. Her father was gone again but promised he would be back in a day or so.

Junior stopped going to school after second grade as Reverend John thought education wasn't that important for his sons. All they needed to know was how to hunt, fish and farm. He needed them at home doing the farm work while he "spread the gospel."

Junior grinned and said, "Howdy Lucy. Did Ms. Alva talk to you about us getting married?"

"Yes she did," answered Lucy, wishing her father had stayed around.

"Well, what do you say?" asked Junior a bit impatiently.

"My Paw says if it is what I want it is alright with him but we have to wait awhile. He says we need to get to know each other better before taking such an important step."

"What's to know, I like you, you like me, that's enough in my book," answered Junior, beginning to feel a little uneasy.

This was not going exactly as he had planned. He too had been doing a lot of thinking. He purposefully put off coming by to see Lucy thinking she would be so worked up with worry by the time he did show up, she would all but jump into his arms with relief at the sight of him.

"Well, Granny Alva said Reverend John was going to give you some land and build a house for us. I thought we could get to know each other a little better while that was being done," said Lucy, a bit surprised at her boldness.

"You want to wait until I build a house girl!" exclaimed Junior, feeling his anger rise. "Why that will take a month at least with the entire family working on it day and night. There's lumber to be cut and hauled, not to mention harvest season is coming up."

Lucy was surprised at his reaction and wondered that maybe she was being a little unreasonable. "Well where would we live until the house is finished if we married before then?" asked Lucy.

"Why, you would just keep living right here and I would keep living at home. We would see each other when we could," answered Junior, kind of warming to that idea. He could come over here and have her when her sisters were gone then go about his business, which could include visiting the Turney sisters over on Peach Orchard Road. They were quite the pair and were pretty free with their affections.

"I don't know about all this," said Lucy. "I have to talk to Granny Alva but I promise I will give you an answer by next Sunday. Granny is coming over after church and I will talk to her then."

"Are you saying you don't want to marry me?" asked Junior indignantly.

"No, I'm not saying I don't want to marry you. I'm just not sure it is a good idea to get married when we hardly know each other." Lucy said, beginning to feel a little uncomfortable.

"All right," Junior said reluctantly, "but I want an answer no later than Sunday."

Junior stamped away without even saying goodbye. Just who did she think she was? He should have just taken her right there and then and forgotten about her, but he knew his daddy would have his hide. Junior knew his father was aware of his visits to the Turney sisters but it would be a different story with Lucy. The religious old fool would be fit to be tied if he found out he had taken a "good girl" like Lucy against her will. Reverend John cared more about public opinion than he did his own family, Junior sometimes thought. The more he thought about it the angrier he became. Oh, he could wait, if that's what it took. But make no mistake, she would pay and pay dearly when the time finally came.

Lucy was afraid she may have blown her chance with Junior. He did not seem very happy about having to wait until their house was built to get married. Greta and Marcy noticed how quiet Lucy was and that she hardly touched her food that night. She usually discussed all the events at school with them over their evening meal, but not tonight. They decided to go to bed early and leave her to her thoughts.

CHAPTER 6

Lucy's father returned earlier than expected the next morning and Lucy breathed a sigh of relief. The girls had already left for school so maybe she would have a chance to talk to him. She had a decision to make and she certainly couldn't make it by herself.

She fixed him a plate of the biscuits and gravy left from breakfast, and as he ate, sat across the table from him. "Paw, Junior came by a couple days ago," she stated hesitantly.

"Oh, and have you made a decision about his marriage proposal?" asked her father.

"Well, I told him what you said about us getting to know each other better. I told him since Reverend John was going to build us a house, we would have plenty of time to spend together."

Lucy's Paw sat quietly eating for a moment then said, "Well, what did he say to that?"

"I don't think he was too happy, Paw. He wants us to go ahead and get married now. He said I could live here and he would still live at home so he would be close by to help with the building of the house."

"Looks to me like that boy is in an awful big hurry to get married," said Lucy's Paw. "I don't know what to tell you Lucy girl. I don't want to see this chance at happiness pass you by but I am not quite sure this boy is right for you. If he has the feelings for you he aught to, he would be willing to wait."

"I know, Paw, but I have a feeling Junior won't wait and I keep thinking of all the things he can offer me. There seems to be no one else interested in me and I hate to let this chance slip by."

Marriage was about the only prospect young girls had in those days. There weren't that many occupations open to women, especially those living in rural areas. It was expected they would marry and bear lots of children to help with the farm work

"Well your Granny Alva is coming over after church Sunday, you can talk to her some more about this. She is wise and can give you better advice than I can."

"Thanks Paw. Now you had better get to bed and get some rest. You look completely tuckered out," said Lucy, with a gentle pat on his back.

"Think I will Lucy. I am not feeling so well. Guess I just need a good night's sleep in my own bed," Lucy's

Paw said, as he slowly rose and left the room. When Lucy's father was away from home his nights were usually spent in some ones barn or hay stack.

Lucy and the girls had taken over the room their parents had shared after their mother's death. Their Paw explained, since he was going to be gone a lot, it only made since they should sleep where they could be warm in the winter.

Lucy awoke Sunday morning to a cloudy, dreary day. The rain had not yet started but the clouds looked as though they would burst wide open any moment. She worried that Granny Alva might not be able to visit her today if the weather was bad. She kept an eye on the sky as she went about her chores. She rushed Greta and Marcy out of the house before breakfast to fetch water from the spring. The spring fed into a little creek which normally was just a trickle. A heavy rain, however, would bring a torrent of water rushing down from the hills above. The flooding usually lasted only a few hours but it was impossible to reach the spring when this occurred.

Lucy hoped they would have a well dug at their new house if she decided to marry Junior. She did not know if she would be allowed to have any input into the construction of the house but suspected she would not.

Lucy's Paw was usually up by now. He would bring the stove wood in for Lucy to have a good supply while he was gone. He had built a crude wood box which sat behind the stove. The wood would be brought in and loaded into the box where it could be kept dry. This was a big help to Lucy as it was very hard to start a fire with wet wood.

The girls returned with their water and still their father had not stirred. Lucy was undecided as to whether to disturb him as he had seemed so tired the night before. When breakfast was ready, however, Lucy became concerned that she still did not hear her father stirring about. She went to the door and called out, "Paw, you up, breakfast is ready." She stood with her ear close to the door. Hearing nothing, Lucy decided to peek in to be sure he was alright.

Lucy could see her father lying on the bed with his back to her. When she called him again, he did not stir. "Paw," Lucy said, as she hesitantly approached the bed. She touched her father on the shoulder and jerked her hand away when she felt how stiff and cold he was. Her heart racing now, Lucy came closer to the bed and looked closely at her father. Shaking, she sank to the floor sobbing as she realized her father was dead.

Hearing Lucy's cries, Greta and Marcy came running into the room but stopped short as Lucy motioned them to stay where they were.

"What's wrong with Paw?" asked little Greta.

Lucy tried to compose herself. For the girls sake she had to pull herself together. Somehow she had to get word to Granny Alva and get some help. She did not want to leave the girls alone at this time but felt she had no other choice.

"Marcy, you are a big girl now and I need you to take care of Greta while I go for help," Lucy said, herding them into the next room.

"But Lucy," cried little Greta, "I am afraid. Can't we go with you?"

Lucy glanced out the window, debating on taking them with her. At that moment, the skies opened and a torrent of rain started coming down. That settled the matter. She would not take the girls out in this weather. She could get to Granny's a lot faster without them.

Lucy gathered little Greta into her arms, trying to relieve her fears. "I need you to be a big girl now Greta. I can't take you out in this rain. I need to get to Granny's as fast as possible and you would only slow me down. You will be fine here with Marcy if you just do what Marcy tells you," she explained.

Lucy glanced at Marcy and saw the uncertainty on her face. "Marcy, why don't you and Greta get out your checker board after breakfast? You don't even have to do the breakfast dishes. We can clean those up when I get back."

This seemed to calm the girl's fears. Lucy got out her Paw's old coat which might repel some of the rain, and with a final glance at her sisters, ran out the door.

She knew it was unlikely anyone would be out on the road in this weather so she had no hopes of getting a ride. It was three miles to Granny Alva's house. Lucy had hopes someone might be at the church, but as she passed by, saw no one in sight. Guess everyone was staying in today, even Reverend John, she thought.

Lucy tried to run but was hindered by the mud in the dirt road. At one point she lost her footing and went sprawling in the mud. By now the coat was completely soaked through. By the time she reached Granny Alva's house, she was exhausted, muddy and soaked to the bone.

She bounded upon the small porch and beat on Granny's door. The door was opened immediately by Uncle Thomas who was shocked to see the drenched Lucy standing there.

"What in the world you doing out here in this weather girl?" asked Uncle Thomas.

The morning's events had taken a toll on Lucy. She burst into tears and sank into her Uncle's arms. Hearing the commotion, Granny Alva came rushing in from the kitchen.

She took Lucy by the hand, slipped the wet coat off her shoulders, and led her to a nearby chair. "Lucy honey, tell me what's wrong," she said, smoothing the wet hair from Lucy's eyes.

"Granny, Paw's dead. He came home last night not feeling well. When I called him this morning for breakfast he did not get up. I went to check on him and he was cold and stiff. He was dead Granny," said Lucy, bursting into tears again.

"There, there Lucy. Granny will take care of everything. What about Marcy and Greta? Are they alright?" she asked, gathering Lucy into her arms.

"They are fine but a little scared to stay by themselves. I didn't know what else to do Granny. I couldn't bring them out in this weather," said Lucy, beginning to get control.

"You did exactly right Lucy."

Turning to Thomas, Granny instructed him to go hitch the mules to the wagon. "Get that old tarp we use to cover the hay. That will give us some protection from the rain. We need to get Lucy back to the girls as soon as possible."

Granny Alva had come to love her son-in-law during the years he had been married to her daughter. He had been good to her Lindy and had loved her dearly. After her death, however, Granny had not approved of the way he had left the girls alone. She tried to understand and help out when ever she could. She could see he was never the same after Lindy's death, but still, the girls needed him and he wasn't there for them.

Granny Alva felt such sadness come over her for her daughter, her son-in-law and her grand children. She was a religious person but sometimes it seemed God punished the good and helped the wicked. She pushed her thoughts aside. She knew she would be needed by the girls for the next few days and she would do what had to be done.

CHAPTER 7

Word of a death spread fast in rural communities. No one knew exactly how as there were very few telephones in the area. On their way back to Lucy's cabin, they had met Mr. Duncan. He was on his way to the Widow Lawrence's for his usual Sunday lunch. He came to a stop, wondering why they were out in this weather in a wagon.

"Howdy folks, what ya'll doing out in this weather?" he asked, spitting a stream of tobacco juice out the window of his truck.

"Lucy's paw passed away last night," answered Thomas. "We have to get over there and take care of the arrangements."

"Sorry to hear about that. Is there anything I can do to help you folks out?" asked Mr. Duncan, real concern in his voice. That was the way with country people. They went about their daily lives, hardly seeing each other, sometimes for days. When they were needed, however, they were there for each other.

"Since you will be going right by Reverend John's house, if you could stop by and ask him to come over to Lucy's cabin, it would be a big help," answered Granny Alva.

"I'll be glad to do that. I am sure the Widow Lawrence will want to bring some food over," answered Mr. Duncan, as he put the truck in gear.

The day went by with a flourish of activities at the cabin. People had been stopping by all afternoon with food and condolences. The rain had stopped and was gone almost as quickly as it had come. The sun was peeking through the clouds now and word was getting out.

Lucy and her sisters stood together accepting the hugs and words of concern as the ladies of the community came and went. They were exhausted but it was expected of them. Lucy could hear the whispers, "What will happen to these poor girls now?" "That Henry was a wanderer but he cared about those girls." After death, people seemed to make excuses for a person's short comings.

Reverend John arrived shortly after Lucy and her family returned home. Mr. Duncan had been kind enough to drive him over. Reverend John had asked Junior to come with him. He felt if Junior was going to marry Lucy, she might need him at this time. Junior, however, was still snuggled up in his feather bed and could not be roused. Reverend John was disappointed in his son but as usual, made excuses for him. He had worked hard in the fields the day before and deserved a little rest, he told himself.

Lucy could not help but notice Junior was not with his father. Surely he should know how upset she was and want to be with her. "Through thick and thin" was what Granny had said about marriage. Well, this was certainly thin, thought Lucy, having more doubts than ever about Junior's sincerity.

Uncle Thomas and some of the men of the community got busy building the box necessary for the burial while others dug the grave. Lucy's father would be buried beside the grave of his beloved wife. He had never told anyone this was what he wanted, but there was no question in anyone's mind.

The wake went on through out the afternoon and night. People would stop by, visit awhile, eat and leave, offering their condolences as they went. Lucy did not need to worry about food as there was more than they could ever eat. There was fried chicken, potato salad, cakes and pies. Lucy and the girls had never seen so much food but for some reason, found they had little appetite.

Bodies had to be buried as soon as possible in those days. The body would start to decompose quickly, especially in warmer weather. Henry's funeral was held the very next day. Lucy dressed the girls and her self in their good dresses and rode with Uncle Thomas to the church. Granny Alva was to ride over with Mr. Duncan who had been wonderful in ferrying everyone about.

What would happen to them now, Lucy kept thinking. She had always taken care of the cooking and such but her father had supplied them with what they needed to survive. Now that he was gone, what would they do?

Junior had finally showed up, mumbled his condolences to Lucy, and headed straight to the food. He had expected his answer from Lucy today but knew his Paw would skin him alive if he approached her at a time like this. His mind was racing, however, as to how he could turn this to his advantage. Lucy would need him more than ever now that her Paw was gone. This could be a good thing he reasoned, and he could wait another day or two.

The body was moved to the church where the coffin sat on display before the people gathered for the funeral. Granny Alva had picked a large bouquet of wild flowers, and placed them on top of the pine box.

Lucy and the girls took their seat beside Granny Alva and felt comforted in her closeness. Reverend John preached a rousing sermon about the consequences of sin and the finality of death.

The body was moved to the cemetery and some of the men filled the grave after the family left. Granny Alva could see the girls were exhausted so she suggested they return to her house and spend the night. She would make pallets on the floor for them. Uncle

Thomas would go to the cabin and return with the leftover food. If not eaten, food spoiled quickly as most people had no refrigeration

Lucy and the girls slept late the next morning. Granny Alva decided to let them sleep while she prepared breakfast. They had some hard decisions to make and she needed time to think. It would be out of the question for the girls to keep living at the cabin by themselves. She could help them as she was able. She knew Thomas would not mind checking on them occasionally but he had his own family to see after. Times were hard and money was scarce. She knew Henry had been gone a lot but he had seen to it the girls necessities were met.

Granny Alva had breakfast on the table and decided it was time to rouse the girls. She looked at them sleeping so peacefully and hated to wake them. There had been more heaped on these little girls than any adult should have to bear. Her heart swelled with love and pride for Lucy as she thought of how she had taken over the household after Lindy's death. She should have been able to go to school and do the things little girls do but had been forced to become an adult at the age of nine. "Lord, help these babies get through these next few weeks," she said, in a low whisper.

The girls rose reluctantly, wiping the sleep from their eyes. They had removed their good dresses and were wearing some of Uncle Thomas's old shirts. Granny Alva did not know why she had saved them. When Thomas had married and moved out, he had left some of his things behind. Granny Alva could not bring herself to throw anything away. Someone might be able to get some use of them sometime, she had reasoned.

To Granny Alva's surprise, the girls ate ravenously. They had hardly eaten the past two days. She guessed the shock of their father's death was wearing off and was grateful. There was still fried chicken from the wake and Granny Alva had made her usual biscuits and gravy. She even allowed the girls to have some of her treasured coffee with a teaspoon of honey for sweetening. She knew this would give them the energy to get through the day.

After the kitchen had been cleaned and the bedding removed from the floor, Granny Alva sat the girls down for the talk she knew they had to have.

"Lucy, we have to think about what is best for you and the girls now that your Paw is gone," she said, watching the girls closely. She did not want to press them on the matter if they were not ready.

"I know Granny," Lucy said, with surprising calm. "I thought about it all day yesterday. I don't know were my marriage proposal from Junior stands. I can't just leave Marcy and Greta alone at the cabin."

"Your whole life has been spent taking care of others Lucy. I know you did what you had to do and I love you dearly for it, but you should not have to give up your chance at happiness now. I must say, however,

I am very disappointed in Junior's actions during this time. If he cares enough to want to marry you, he should have been more attentive in your time of need," reasoned Granny Alva.

"I know Granny. I don't understand his actions either. Maybe boys think different from girls and he did not realize I needed him," Lucy said, wondering why she felt the need to defend Junior.

"Well we need to see where he stands on his proposal first I guess. The question is, Lucy, do you still feel you want to marry him?"

Granny Alva had been doing a lot of thinking and had come up with a solution but she did not want to influence Lucy's decision. Marcy was getting older and would be starting a family of her own soon. She would soon be fifteen years old. Girls married young in those days and she was sure Marcy would be no exception. Like Lucy, she resembled her mother and had the same dark beauty. She had decided that if Lucy wanted to marry Junior, she would take the girls in herself. She could set up beds in Thomas' old room and felt they would be as comfortable there as they had been in the cabin.

Granny Alva's house was small but still larger than the girl's cabin. She had used Thomas' old bedroom to set up her quilting frames. She made the most beautiful quilts and got Mr. Johnson to sell them on commission along his "rolling store" route. She saved every little piece of fabric she could get her hands on and used them to make the intricate patterns on her quilts. It had gotten harder for her to do the fancy needle work lately, however, as her hands were becoming stiff with arthritis. Maybe she could teach the girls how to help her with the most detailed work, she thought.

She had left the quilting frames lowered to chair level as the bedroom was not being used. If the girls decided to stay with her, she would raise the frames to the ceiling and lower them whenever needed.

With a promise she would be by to see them the next morning, Granny Alva instructed Thomas to take them home. She hoped maybe Junior would go by to see Lucy if she went home. Once they knew of his intentions, they could get together and make a decision about the girl's future.

Uncle Thomas dropped them off and went on his way. He promised Lucy he would see to the wood supply when he brought Granny Alva over the next day.

Lucy and the girls changed out of their good dresses as there were chores to be done. They had brought with them some of the left over food so lunch preparation would not be necessary. Marcy and Greta had just left, a pail in each hand, to fetch water from the spring when Lucy heard a knock at the door. She felt her heart give a leap as she saw Junior standing there.

"Hoped I'd find you at home," said Junior. "Came by yesterday afternoon but you were not here. I was

wondering if you'd made your mind up about us getting married."

"I haven't had time to do a lot of thinking about it,
what with Paw dying and all," said Lucy.

"Well you promised me an answer today. I've been
giving it a lot of thought. Looks like you're gonna be
needing some body around here with your Paw gone,"
Junior said, trying not to show his impatience.

Junior had indeed been thinking about it a lot. There
wouldn't be any excuse now. They could live in Lucy's
cabin until the house could be built on his land. That
little Marcy was getting older and was a real looker. If
he played his cards right he could have them both.

"I know I promised Junior, but I have to consider the
girls now with Paw gone. I can't just up and leave them
by themselves," Lucy said, hoping she could make him
understand.

"I've already thought about that," said Junior, sounding real pleased with himself. "We can just live right
here until our house is built. I am sure daddy will
understand that you need me around to help with the
chores, what with your Paw gone."

Junior thought this was a great plan. He would not
have to help with the harvesting as much if he had to
be at Lucy's. Reverend John was a stickler for "doing
unto others as you would have them do unto you."
Junior knew if he planned it just right he could get out

of the hardest work. His brothers would not be too pleased but that did not concern him.

"That doesn't sound unreasonable, but I would still like to discuss this with Granny Alva. She had not thought about them starting their married life there in the cabin with the girls present. She guessed it would be the sensible thing to do, however.

"All right Junior, come by tomorrow afternoon and the decision will be made," Lucy told him, hoping she was not making things too difficult.

"I'll be here, but mind you, I want a final answer by then," Junior said, itching to get his hands on her. He did not know what it was about her that kept him so riled up. He did not like to be told no and he did not like to be kept waiting. Maybe that was the attraction. That would soon be taken care of, he thought, as he trotted away on his old mule.

True to her word, Granny Alva came by the next morning by ten O'clock. She could have been there earlier but hoped the girls would sleep in awhile. She was sure they were exhausted from the past days events.

Lucy was up at dawn, however. She had tossed and turned all night and had finally gotten up, knowing she had to be disturbing her sisters. She could think of nothing but Junior and the decision she had to make. She hoped Granny could help her sort it all out.

"Good morning Granny," Lucy said, opening the door.

"Hello Lucy dear.   How are you and the girls this morning?"   Marcy and Greta came forward to give their Granny a kiss on the cheek.

"We are fine Granny. I am glad you came early. Junior is coming over this afternoon and I have to give him an answer," said Lucy.

Marcy pulled a chair over for her Granny. She and Greta went about cleaning up the breakfast dishes leaving Lucy and Granny Alva to talk.

"He wants us to get married now and live right here in the cabin with the girls. He says we can do that until our house is built, which is not unreasonable I suppose," Lucy said, pulling up a chair of her own.

"How do you feel about that really, Lucy?" asked Granny Alva.

"Well I hardly envisioned starting my married life with the girls still in tow but I can't see leaving them by them selves either," said Lucy, feeling a little guilty.

"Lucy girl, I may have the solution," said Granny Alva. "I have given this a lot of thought and I want you to hear me out before you say anything. You know I have that extra room now that your Uncle Thomas is married and gone. I've just been using it for my quilting but that can be taken care of easily. What do you think about Marcy and Greta coming to live with me?" asked Granny Alva.

Upon hearing their names, Marcy and Greta moved a little closer to the conversation. It would not be so bad living with Granny Alva. She always seemed to have plenty of food and her house was actually closer to the school house than their cabin.

"Why Granny, that is a wonderful idea," said Lucy, knowing Marcy and Greta would probably love living with their Granny. She also knew they would be well taken care of.

"Lucy, it is hard enough starting a new marriage with just the two of you. It would be doubly hard if you have children in the house to take care of. Junior may say he doesn't mind now, but that could, and probably would change after awhile. I want you to have the best opportunity to make this work."

"How do you girls feel about this?" Granny Alva asked, turning to Marcy and Greta.

"Of course we would miss Lucy something fierce, Granny, but we would love to come live with you," said Marcy, glancing at Lucy.

"We would be a big help to you too Granny," chimed in little Greta.

"I know you would dears," said Granny. "Then it's settled. Lucy you can tell your young man you are ready, if it is what you want," Granny Alva stressed.

The next few hours were spent making plans. Once Lucy and Junior had set a date for the wedding, Granny Alva would have Uncle Thomas come over with the wagon for the girls things.

Lucy did not know, but Granny Alva had been preparing a "hope chest" for her for several years. She had two of her beautiful quilts and two soft feather pillows made from chicken feathers plucked over the years. There was a set of dish towels and bathing towels on which she had embroidered tiny pink flowers. There was a set of sheets she had ordered from the Sears & Roebuck catalog. She had also made the most beautiful gown for Lucy made of soft white flannel. She had adorned it with ribbons and pink flowers embroidered around the neck. She wanted Lucy to feel special on her wedding night.

Granny's husband, Big Tom, as everyone had called him, had died several years earlier. He had worked for the railroad and when he died Granny was able to draw a portion of his pension. Therefore, she could live a little more comfortably than some of her neighbors.

"Lucy, there are a few things I want to give you before you get married. I will bring them over when we come to pick up the girls," said Granny Alva, noticing Lucy's surprise. "We also have to get busy making you a wedding dress. If it is alright with you, we can adjust Dottie's wedding dress to fit you." Dottie was Thomas' wife and Granny Alva had already spoken to her about

the dress. Dottie was very fond of Lucy and was happy
to have her wear it.

"Oh Granny, are you sure she won't mind?" exclaimed
Lucy, remembering the beautiful white dress Dottie
had worn when she married Uncle Thomas.

"I have already spoken to her and she is pleased you
would want to wear it," said Granny Alva, rising slowly
from her chair. The arthritis in her knees was getting worse. Maybe it would be a good thing having
the girls with her to help out, she thought. There
were other things she knew she should talk to Lucy
about. She knew Lucy knew nothing of what would
be expected of her on her wedding night. Granny
wanted to prepare her but thought they could have
their talk after Lucy had spoken to Junior.

Junior was at the cabin shortly after noon the next day.
Lucy was on her way to the hen house when she saw
him coming down the road. He seems to be in a good
mood, Lucy thought, as he bounded off his horse.

"Hey there Lucy girl, you headed to the hen house?"
said Junior, noticing the basked in her hand.

"Yes, we forgot to fetch the eggs yesterday so I imagine
there is a goodly supply today," said Lucy, stopping for
him to catch up.

"Then it can wait a few more minutes," he said, catching up to her and pulling her down on a nearby log.
Lucy's Paw had been sawing the log up for fire wood.

A goodly portion of it was still left and made a good seat.

"Did you talk to Ms. Alva about us getting married and all?" asked Junior.

"Yes I did, and it has been decided that the girls will go live with her once we are married," said Lucy, thinking this would please Junior. She was confused though when she saw the slightest frown cross his face.

Junior was more than a little disappointed. He had begun to warm to the idea of having that little Marcy living under the same roof with them. You would have thought a preacher's son would never think such things, but Junior seemed to have no moral compass at all.

"Guess that would be best, although I really don't mind if they want to stay here," said Junior. He noticed how pretty Lucy looked with her hair blowing in the breeze. She was sure a looker, he thought, and before long she would be his.

"Well, guess it's settled then. We'll get married as soon as I can get the license." It never occurred to Junior that he should ask Lucy about her ideas or plans for the wedding. He just wanted it done the quickest, easiest way possible.

Lucy rose and said, "Guess I had better get those eggs now." She was feeling a little unsettled and wanted to be alone to think.

Lucy spent the rest of the day gathering the few belongings the girls had in preparation for their move. She was excited but there was also an underlying current of dread. She could not shake the feeling that something was not quite right. She and the girls chatted about the wedding and what their role might be. Lucy had no idea about planning a wedding. She knew Granny Alva would be there to help guide her through it all. She assumed she and Junior would be married in his father's church and Preacher John would perform the ceremony. She had only been to one wedding, that of her Uncle Thomas and she thought it a beautiful ceremony.

Lucy arose early the next morning in anticipation of the girls move. She wanted to have everything ready when Granny Alva and Uncle Thomas got there. The girls were excited about this change in their lives but felt a little guilty about leaving Lucy.

They had just finished cleaning the breakfast dishes when Granny Alva arrived. She brought with her all the wonderful things she had promised Lucy. She wanted Lucy to have the items now so she could prepare the cabin before the wedding. The new bedding was a God send to Lucy as what she had was completely threadbare. Granny Alva also brought with her Dottie's wedding dress for Lucy to try on. Lucy had never looked so beautiful Granny Alva thought, as she stood back and admired her. The dress would only need minor alterations as Lucy and Dottie were close in size.

Before leaving Granny Alva asked Lucy to take a walk with her down by the creek. It was a nice warm day with not a cloud in the sky. They strolled down the path worn bare by the many trips the girls made fetching water. Granny Alva stopped and sank down on a huge stump left from a giant tree cut down many years before. Lucy sat down beside her.

"Lucy, I wish your mother was here to have this talk with you. I am sure she could do much better than I at explaining things to you. At any rate, when a man and woman get married certain things will be expected of you. Love between a man and woman can be a beautiful thing if you both care about each other's feelings. You will be expected to do things on your wedding night which can be a little freighting and a little painful. That will pass and you will come to love your husband's touch. A good wife always tries to please her husband." Granny Alva paused and looked at Lucy.

"Do you have any questions you would like to ask me Lucy?"

Lucy stared at her hands clasped tightly in her lap. She had all kinds of questions but did not know exactly what they were.

"Well Granny, Junior has kissed me a couple of times and it wasn't like I thought it was going to be. It was a bit rough and it scared me a little," said Lucy shyly.

"Junior is still quite young and a bit overly passionate I fear. I am sure after you are married and he knows you will always be there for him, he will settle down and make a pleasing husband for you. Life is hard Lucy, as you well know. If you put your mind and heart in it, I know you can make a good life for you and Junior."

Granny Alva rose and taking Lucy's hand in hers pulled her to her feet.

"I assume you will be married at the church with Reverend John performing the ceremony. You will look so beautiful in your dress Lucy. I will make you a bouquet of wild flowers and tie them with white ribbons just as I did for Dottie," said Granny Alva feeling younger than she had in some time.

"Now let's get back to the cabin before those girls come looking for us. They are truly going to miss you Lucy. Hopefully, we will still see you quite often. I will stop in to see you as often as your Uncle Thomas has the time. These old legs are not what they used to be so I have to rely on Thomas to transport me about."

"I love you Granny, thank you for everything," said Lucy, flinging her arms around the older woman's neck.

Granny Alva and the girls left that afternoon leaving Lucy to get about the business of preparing the cabin for her new life. She scrubbed everything in sight and put the new linens on the bed. She did not want to soil them before her wedding night so decided to sleep in the girl's bed. This would be the first night she had spent in the cabin alone. She feared she might be afraid and unable to sleep. She need not have worried, however, she was so exhausted from all the excitement and cleaning, she fell asleep immediately. Little did she know, that would be her last night of peaceful sleep for years to come.

CHAPTER 8

Lucy arose the next morning rested and refreshed. She spent the morning going about her normal chores too excited to eat. The cabin looked nicer than it had ever looked. Lucy moved the girl's bed into the room where her father had slept. Granny Alva had brought her an old rocking chair saying she would need it to rock the babies she and Junior would have. Lucy made a cushion of rose colored print and sat the rocker in the corner where the girl's bed had sat. She gathered some of the wild roses and placed them in a fruit jar for the kitchen table.

Around noon Lucy stood and admired her handy work, quite pleased with the result. She had just sat down for a bite of lunch when there came a knock at the door. She was quite surprised to see Junior standing there with a wide grin.

"Guess what I got," said Junior, holding out a piece of paper.

"Why Junior, I wasn't expecting you for a few days," Lucy said, reaching for the paper.

"It's that marriage license you wanted. Now we can get hitched," Junior said, as he pulled her down on the top step.

"That's great Junior, but I am surprised you were able to get one so quickly."

"Well Mr. Johnson gave me a ride over to the court house this morning and here I am. Daddy is going to be leaving this afternoon for a funeral he has to preach over at Grand Junction. If we leave right now we can catch him before he leaves," said Junior, sounding very pleased with his self.

Lucy was shocked and just stood there with her mouth open for a moment. What about her wedding with the beautiful dress she was to wear? What about Granny and the girls? She wanted them to be there for one of the most important days of her life.

"Junior, we can't just go get married right now. I thought we would get married in the church. Why Granny has brought me the most beautiful dress to wear and I wanted her and the girls to be there."

Junior was seething inside but knew he had to handle this calmly. He took Lucy's hand and sweetly told her how much he loved her and could not wait another day to be with her. He explained his father would be gone for five days. He had a funeral he was doing in the next county and would be going on to preach the revival for a neighboring church afterwards.

"This is important to me Lucy. I want my father to marry us but he is going to be gone and I don't want us to wait until he comes back. Please do this for me. I promise you, we will repeat our vows in the church on our first wedding anniversary and you can wear your beautiful dress then."

Lucy was so confused and could not think straight. She knew Granny Alva and the girls would be so disappointed if they could not be there but she had to think of Junior now and what he wanted. Lucy had grown accustomed to putting other people before herself, so she agreed. It was decided they would leave right then and Junior's father could marry them right there in their living room, with Ms. Allie as witness.

Lucy changed into her Sunday dress. She was thankful she had bathed and washed her hair that morning. This wasn't exactly what she had dreamed about but Junior had promised she would have her day on their anniversary.

Lucy and Junior had hardly gotten a mile down the road when they met Reverend John. Junior's older brother had purchased an old truck with the help of his father and in return was given the responsibility of ferrying the Reverend about. Junior stopped the wagon and told his father they were on their way to get him to marry them.

"I can't turn around and go back home now, boy. I am already running late," said Reverend John, glancing at Lucy uncertainly.

"But we can't wait until you come back daddy. Lucy needs someone there with her at the cabin as the girls have already moved in with Ms. Alva," Junior said. He knew if he appealed to his father's charitable nature he would get further.

"Tell you what I will do Junior. If Lucy is agreeable, I will just marry you right here and now if you have the license with you. Carl here can be your witness. I know it is not your ideal situation but it will still get the job done," said Reverend John.

"What do you say Lucy? It really won't matter who the witness is. This way Daddy can go about his business and we can go about ours," Junior said, patting Lucy's hand in reassurance.

Lucy was near tears but did not want Junior or the Reverend to see. She was so disappointed Granny Alva and her sisters were not gong to be at her wedding. Now she was being told they should get married right there in the middle of the road. This all felt terribly wrong to Lucy but as always, she put others needs before hers and agreed with a whispered, "OK."

Junior helped Lucy from the wagon and they both stood before Reverend John and repeated their wedding vows. Junior's brother remained sitting behind the steering wheel looking quite amused about the whole thing. In a matter of minutes Junior and Lucy were married. With a quick peck on Lucy's cheek and a "welcome to the family Lucy," Reverend John and Carl left, appearing happy to be on their way.

"Well we did it," said Junior, as he began to turn the wagon around.

"Where are we going?" asked Lucy. "Don't you need to go get some of your things?"

"I can take care of that later. We have more important things to take care of right now," Junior said, as he squeezed Lucy's leg.

Lucy's heart was racing as Junior rushed the mules back to the cabin. What would be expected of her when they reached the cabin? Would she be given time to change into the gown Granny Alva had made for her? This was not at all how she had dreamed her wedding night would be. First of all, it was the middle of the afternoon and she still had chores to do. By the time they reached the cabin Lucy could hardly move from freight and dread.

"Come on girl. What you waiting on?" said Junior, practically dragging her out of the wagon.

Junior closed the door behind them, grabbed Lucy around the waist and spun her around. He was on her before she could push him away, ripping the buttons from her dress as he tore it from her shoulders.

"Please Junior, I have a gown," Lucy tried to tell him, as he drug her towards the bed.

Junior appeared not to hear her. His face was red and his breath was coming in short gasps. Lucy tried to struggle but was no match for Junior. He was quick and brutal with no affection at all. When it was over Lucy lay whimpering, feeling as though her whole body ached. The bed she had so lovingly prepared earlier was now a rumpled mess. The lovely sheets Granny Alva had given her were now blood stained and soiled from Junior's work boots. He had not taken the time to remove them. Her one good dress lay in a torn, crumpled ball on the floor.

"Now get this straight," Junior said, with his finger in Lucy's face. "You belong to me now and you will do what I tell you. All these weeks you been making my life miserable, acting like some goody two shoes. All the waiting and it was hardly worth it, if you want to know the truth. I've had lots better, but you will learn, count on it. Now get up and clean this mess up. I'm going after my things and I want supper on the table when I come back. We will have another go round later. Maybe you can put a little more effort into it next time," Junior said, as he stomped out of the cabin, pulling his pants up as he went.

Lucy lay there as if stunned. What had happened to her? Was this the way married life was for everyone? Was this the way it was going to be for her from now on? The tears were streaming down her face now and she groaned in despair. My God, what had she gotten herself into?

When Junior returned with his belongings, Lucy could not bring herself to look at him. She had washed her new sheets and had them hanging on the clothes line.

She had crawled into the tub herself afterwards and scrubbed until her skin felt raw. Still she felt dirty and sore. She had put her old sheets back on the bed and had lovingly hung her dress up, hoping she might be able to repair the mess Junior had made of it. She had prepared supper using the little she had to work with and hoped it would be acceptable to Junior.

Junior still had not said a word since returning. He went about the business of putting his things away without once asking Lucy where he should put them. When he was finished, he sat down at the table with his arms folded across his chest.

"Well, where is my supper? I've had a hard day and I'm hungry," Junior said.

Lucy did not reply but put a plate before him. She dished up the salt pork, collard greens and corn bread she had prepared. She knew it probably wasn't as good as what he had been use to at Ms. Allies' but it was the best she could do. She had no appetite herself so she busied herself cleaning up the kitchen area.

"Ain't you gonna eat?" asked Junior, sullenly.

"I am not hungry," replied Lucy, without looking at him.

"Well you had better eat cause I got plans for you later," Junior said, with a tone that told Lucy exactly what he meant.

CHAPTER 9

And so it went. Lucy's days were spent in exhaustion and fear knowing what was coming when Junior returned home.

Granny Alva had come by the cabin the day after Lucy and Junior were married. She had come to discuss the wedding plans with Lucy not knowing the deed had already been done. She was shocked when Lucy opened the door. There were dark circles under her eyes, her hair was a mess and there were bruises on her upper arms.

"Why child, what is ever the matter?" Granny Alva exclaimed, as she put her arms around Lucy's shoulders. The whole ugly story came rushing out as Lucy sobbed in her Grandmother's arms. Lucy's Grandmother was so angry she did not realize how hard she was holding Lucy until she heard a small whimper among the sobs.

"You will not stay in this place another day with that man," said Granny Alva, barley able to speak. "You will come home with me today. You can sleep with me if necessary."

Lucy was gathering her things when Junior came bounding through the door. He did not know Ms. Alva was there as Thomas had dropped her off, with the promise of picking her up in an hour. He stopped short when he saw her. He looked around the cabin and saw the things Lucy was stuffing into a flour sack. Realizing her intentions, his face became beet red and his hands clinched into fists at his side.

"Just where do you think you are going?" Junior asked, looking from Ms. Alva to Lucy.

"She's coming home with me," answered Granny Alva, straightening her spine. "I will not have my Granddaughter mistreated by you or anyone else."

"Is that so? Well you listen to me Old Woman. We are married now. She is my wife and she is staying right here with me," said Junior, grabbing Lucy by the arm.

Lucy cried out in pain as Junior twisted her arm.

"Let her go this instant. You are a sorry excuse of a man and a poor excuse for a husband. As soon as Thomas gets back, Lucy will be leaving with us and she won't be coming back."

"We will see about that," said Junior as he reached for his shot gun standing in the corner. "I will blow anyone's head off who tries to take her away from here. She is my wife and here she will stay."

Junior wondered why he was getting so riled up. Lucy had been a big disappointment to him in the bedroom area. Still he was not going to be outdone by this old biddy or her sniveling excuse of a son. He would deal with Lucy later.

Granny Alva heard Thomas pull into the yard and was sorely afraid of what Junior would do. She could see he was very angry, still she did not want to leave Lucy alone with him.

Lucy heard her Uncle also. She looked at her Granny standing so bravely and strong on her behalf. She would die if anything happened to her. She had seen already just how brutal Junior could be. She knew she had to do something or someone could get hurt.

"Junior is right, Granny. We are married now, for better or worse, so why don't you and Uncle Thomas go on home. I will see you in a few days."

Hearing this, Junior let go of her arm. Maybe she was coming to her senses after all. He still held onto the shotgun, however, as he walked to peep out the window.

"Go for now Granny," whispered Lucy. "I can come later when he is not here."

She did not want to leave Lucy alone with this monster but realized she had no choice at the moment. Someone could get hurt, even Lucy.

"I will leave for now but I will be back to check on Lucy in a few days. I am sure Reverend John would be interested in how you and Lucy are doing. I will be sure to let him know the next time I see him," Granny Alva said, hoping that would put a scare into him.

Junior continued to watch out the window until Ms. Alva and her son had gone. Slowly he turned to Lucy and stood glaring at her. Granny Alva's courage in standing up to Junior had given Lucy the strength she needed to face him, and she stared back.

Junior was a bit perplexed by this new Lucy but knew he had the upper hand. He approached her and before Lucy knew what was happening, slapped her hard across the face. Lucy, reeling from the blow, slumped into the nearby rocker with her hand to her cheek.

"You hear me and hear me good," whispered Junior, his rancid breath blowing into Lucy's face. You are not going anywhere. Just to be sure that old bitch doesn't come meddling around here again when I am gone, you will be going to the field with me from now on. You can work out there in the heat right along side me. Maybe that will get some of the sass out of you."

True to his word, the next morning before the sun was up, Junior pushed Lucy out of bed with orders to "get a move on." "You're going with me today and I need my breakfast before we hit the fields." With that, he turned over and went back to sleep.

Thankfully, Lucy still had a little wood left for the stove. She did not know what she would do when that ran out. She had no hopes that Junior would take care of that responsibility as her father and Uncle Thomas had.

Lucy was exhausted from the previous day's events and Junior had shown her no mercy after they had gone to bed. His love making was furious and brutal leaving Lucy aching, with silent tears streaming down her face. Still, she feared what might happen if she did not do as he asked. She rose from the bed and dressed, dreading the day ahead.

"What's she doing here?" asked Carl, seeing Lucy at the end of the cotton row. It was customary in Junior's family for the women to stay at home and take care of the cooking and other household chores.

"Oh she couldn't stand to be away from me so I told her she could help out with the picking." Ain't that right Lucy?" said Junior, with a look that dared her to speak otherwise.

Lucy did not reply but simply bent over the cotton row and started the back breaking task of filling the cotton sack Junior had handed her. She had not done this kind of work before. By the day's end, her back was aching and her hands were bleeding from the prickly cotton boles.

Lucy said not a word as she and Junior rode the wagon home. The back of the wagon was loaded with the cotton they had picked that day. It would be taken to the cotton gin the next day where it would be made into bales and sold. Lucy hoped she would be left alone since they would not be working in the fields and she would not be needed. She would leave for Granny Alva's just as soon as Junior left. She felt once she was safely at her grandmother's house, Junior would not be able to harm her. Granny Alva had her own shotgun and knew how to use it.

Much to Lucy's surprise, however, Junior informed her she would be riding with him and his brother's to the cotton gin.

"But Junior, I have chores to do here. The washing has to be done, there's wood and water to be fetched," said Lucy, trying not to show her disappointment.

"You can do that when we get home this evening and I don't want to hear any more about it," Junior said, as he went out the door to hitch up the wagon. He suspected what Lucy was up to and swore it would not happen if he had to kill her. His obsession for Lucy had changed from one of sexual desire to a will of wits. She would not best him, ever, at anything.

Lucy was embarrassed to be seen in public in her present condition. She had not had time to bath or wash her hair. Her cheek still showed the bruise from Junior's blow two days before. Her feet were sun burned and swollen from walking barefoot down the cotton rows. She could not wear her good shoes to work in the fields and had no others to wear. Her dress was soiled and wrinkled from her day in the field. She had two dresses for everyday wear and her good Sunday dress. Since she had not been able to do laundry, she had no choice but to wear the dress again.

Lucy sat in stoic silence with her head bowed as the wagon was pulled up to the cotton gin. She prayed no one would take note of her but there was little chance of that. With the exception to children, who enjoyed accompanying their father to the gin, women were seldom seen there.

Lucy was startled out of her reverie when she heard her Uncle Thomas say, "Lucy is that you girl?"

She slowly raised her head and could see the shocked look that came over his face.

"My god Lucy, what has happened to you?" asked Uncle Thomas, as he reached for Lucy's hand.

Lucy could feel the tears brim her eyes but knew she had to keep control. Junior had put his shotgun under the wagon seat with a smug look at Lucy before leaving the cabin.

"I am alright Uncle Thomas. I worked in the field yesterday helping Junior and haven't had time to clean myself up," Lucy said, feeling her cheeks turn red.

"What happened to your face?" asked Thomas, taking Lucy's cheek in his hand.

Before Lucy could answer, Junior appeared beside the wagon.

"Get away from this wagon," said Junior. "I'm next in line to go through the gin. With that, he jumped upon the wagon and shook the reigns to move the mules forward.

"Hold on a minute, Junior. I want to know what's been happening with my niece. She looks terrible and there is a bruise on her cheek," said Thomas, walking along side the wagon.

Junior, sensing a confrontation, reached below the seat and brought the shotgun to rest between his knees.

Seeing the gun, Lucy felt she had to do something. Had she known Junior better, she probably would have stood up for herself, but at this point, in her mind she was sure Junior would not hesitate to use the gun.

"Please, Uncle Thomas, I am all right. Tell Granny Alva and the girls I said hello and I hope to see them soon," Lucy said, hoping her Uncle would understand and walk away.

With that, Junior pulled the wagon forward where the cotton would be sucked into the gin and processed into bales after the removal of the seeds. Thomas was left standing with a worried look on his face and little idea as to how to help Lucy. He would go by and discuss the matter with his mother on his way home. They had to figure out a way to get Lucy away from Junior without anyone getting hurt.

Seeing that he had gotten his bluff in on Thomas, Junior turned to Lucy and asked, "what did you say to him?"

"I swear I did not say anything except that I was doing fine," said Lucy.

With that Junior placed his hand on Lucy's leg and pinched so hard Lucy doubled over in pain.

"See that you keep it that way if you care about the bunch of idiots you call relatives," Junior said.

CHAPTER 10

Thomas was worried sick about Lucy. He knew he had to be careful about what he told his mother. When it came to her Granddaughters, she would do anything to protect them, even if it meant her own safety.

Granny Alva knew something was amiss the minute Thomas walked in the door. The girl's were still at school for which he was grateful. There was no need to bring them into this and have them upset.

"What's wrong Thomas?" Granny Alva asked, as she poured him a glass of fresh lemonade.

"I just saw Lucy, Mama, and she did not look well at all. He did not want to tell her about the bruise on her cheek. She looked exhausted and was filthy with sweat and dirt. You know that is not like Lucy."

"Where did you see her Thomas?" asked Granny Alva, anxiously.

"She was at the cotton gin, of all places. Junior was there running his cotton through the gin. He had Lucy with him."

"Why was she at the cotton gin with him?" Granny Alva asked, beginning to get a bad feeling.

"I didn't have a chance to talk to her but a minute when Junior walked up. He pretty much threatened me with that shot gun of his."

"Did Lucy get a chance to say anything to you?"

"Well, she said to tell you and the girl's hello and she hoped to see you soon. If you ask me, that Junior is mistreating her but I don't know what we can do about it for the moment," Thomas said, finishing his lemonade.

"I know what I am going to do about it," said Granny Alva. "As soon as Reverend John returns home, I intend to pay him a little visit. If anyone can straighten that boy out it will be his father."

"Mama, promise me you won't do anything rash. As much as we may want to help Lucy, our hands are pretty much tied. Maybe the opportunity will come along and we can get her away from there. I suspect that is why he is taking Lucy everywhere with him. He probably figures she will leave him if she gets the chance, if indeed, he is mistreating her."

"It breaks my heart to think of Lucy in this situation. I blame myself to a degree. I should have given this more thought before advising Lucy. She had no way of knowing what she was getting into but I suspected. I hoped and prayed I was wrong. I kept telling myself she deserved a chance at happiness. I hoped that Junior was just young and rambunctious and would settle down once he and Lucy were married. I never dreamed he would actually mistreat her," said Granny Alva, with regret in her voice.

"Well, we can only pray his daddy will put the fear of god into him. I am afraid the harm may have been done to Lucy already, however." With that, Thomas rose to leave. "I will be back in a couple of days to take you over to Reverend Johns."

Granny Alva felt so helpless and curling her knotty hands into small fists, she shook them in the air, wailing, "Why God, why?" Falling to her knees, she prayed for Lucy and asked God to keep her Granddaughter safe until she could do something to help her.

The next day was Saturday and Junior announced they would be taking the day off. Lucy was to spend the day taking care of the chores she had let go and "cleaning herself up," as Junior had put it. Telling her she smelled to high heaven. The smell had not bothered him during the night, however, as he had awakened Lucy time after time for sex. Lucy still had not worn the lovely gown Granny Alva had given her. She thought why bother. It would be an insult to Granny wearing it under these circumstances. It was to have been worn for a special, loving occasion. Lucy feared she would never know that kind of love now.

CHAPTER 11

Granny Alva attended church services Sunday with the hopes she would see Lucy there. She assumed she would be attending church with Junior as Reverend John always had his children in church. This Sunday, however, there was no Junior and no Lucy.

Granny Alva made up her mind. She would approach Reverend John after the service and ask if she could come by for a visit that afternoon. She knew it would be a difficult situation to discuss as no parent likes to hear bad things about their children, but it had to be done.

As expected, Reverend John and Ms. Allie said they would love to have Granny Alva come by for a visit, thinking it was purely a social call.

Granny Alva and Ms Allie were settled in the porch swing while Reverend John occupied the lone rocking chair.

"Glad you could come by for a visit, Ms. Alva. Now that our kids are wed guess we will be seeing more of each other," said Reverend John.

"Well I hope so," said Ms. Alva, knowing she had to be careful how she handled this delicate situation. "I noticed Junior was not in church today and wondered if you had seen him or Lucy since you returned from your trip."

"No, I got in late last evening and haven't seen any of the kids. I was disappointed they weren't in church this morning. I am sure you were disappointed Lucy did not get married in the church but they seemed to be bent on getting married. I guess it don't matter where as long as the deed is legal," said Reverend John, not suspecting anything was wrong.

"Yes, I have to admit I was disappointed. I know Lucy had her heart set on it. Which brings up the reason for my visit," said Granny Alva, leaning forward, tensing for a fight. "I have good reason to believe that Junior is mistreating Lucy. If it is not stopped now, it will only get worse."

"What do you mean, mistreating her? They have only been married a few days. What could possibly go wrong in a few days?" asked Reverend John, indignantly. Ms. Allie's back straightened and she unconsciously leaned away from Ms. Alva.

Granny Alva sensed she might have a fight on her hands. She knew Ms. Allie doted on Junior and should have known she would not accept that her son could do any wrong.

"I saw it with my own eyes. Your son practically raped Lucy the minute they got back home after you married them. I went by to discuss the wedding with her, not knowing they were already married, and about fainted when I saw Lucy. She was a wreck and looked awful. I was going to take her home with me and your son threatened me and Thomas with a shotgun," Granny Alva said, pausing to catch her breath.

"We were ordered out of the house and told not to return. He has been making Lucy go with him every where, even working in the fields. Thomas saw her a couple of days ago at the cotton gin. Junior even made her go to the gin with him. Thomas said she was dirty, exhausted and had a big bruise on her cheek. Again, Junior threatened him with his shotgun if he interfered. Thomas said Lucy appeared to be terrified of Junior." Running out of breath, Granny Alva stopped and waited for a response from Junior's parents.

Reverend John just sat there for a moment staring at Granny Alva as if she had lost her mind. Ms. Allie's face was red with anger and Granny Alva suspected it was not directed at Junior.

"Sounds like you and Thomas are meddling in something that is none of your concern. I suspect that little Lucy may be a bit head strong as she has had little adult supervision most of her life. I know we have spoiled Junior a bit but he would never hit a woman. If he is taking Lucy with him, maybe it is because she wants to be with him. Did you think of that?"

"And maybe, he is taking her with him because he knows Lucy will leave him given the chance because he is mistreating her," said Granny Alva, gritting her teeth for control.

"I will talk to the boy, if it will make you feel better. But I know my boy and I think you and Thomas would do well to stay out of their affairs and let them work it out themselves," said Reverend John, rising as if to say the conversation was over.

Thomas had left Granny Alva to talk to the Reverend by herself, at her request, but promised he would not be far away and would return quickly. He suspected the meeting would not go well as everyone knew how spoiled Junior was.

Thankfully, Thomas pulled up in front of the house just as Reverend John disappeared inside. Ms. Alva suspected what Reverend John had to say would be nothing compared to Ms. Allie, judging from the look on her face.

"I am sorry if I have upset you Ms. Allie. No one likes to hear bad things about their children but I can't stand by and see Lucy hurt. She doesn't deserve that kind of treatment. You know what a hard life she has had and I think deep down you know I am telling the truth. I hope Reverend John can talk some sense into Junior, but if he can't, I will not let this rest. Good day Ms. Allie"

And with that Ms. Alva walked away, leaving Junior's mother to sit and fume.

True to his word, Reverend John went to the fields where his son's were working the next day. He was surprised to see Lucy there, struggling to fill her cotton sack. Junior, seeing his father, dropped his sack and went forward to meet him at the edge of the field.

Passing Lucy, he hissed under his breath, "keep your mouth shut and remember you are out here because you want to be here."

Junior and his father sat in the shade where Junior picked up the communal water jug and drank deeply.

"What you doing out here daddy? Did you have a good trip?" said Junior, playing his father as he always did.

"I came out to have a talk with you Junior. What is Lucy doing out here in the field with you? You know it is the tradition of the women in our family to do the chores at home and bear us our children. It doesn't look good for you to have her out here working. Doesn't she have things to do at home?"

"Oh, I told her that Daddy but she insists she wants to work right along side me. Says she can't stand to be apart from me," boasted Junior.

"Is that so," said Reverend John. "Maybe you wouldn't mind calling Lucy in for a minute. Look's as if she could use a little rest."

Junior was reluctant to have his father talk to Lucy as he was not sure what she would say but felt he had no choice, and called out to her.

"Lucy, come here and have a rest with me and Daddy for a minute," called Junior sweetly.

Lucy was glad for the break but hated for Reverend John to see her in this condition. Thankfully, Junior had allowed her to get a bath and do the laundry the day before so she had on clean clothes. At least they had been when the day had started. Now, however, she was soaked with sweat. Her hair was stringing down her face and her feet were dirty and cracking from the sunburn. Approaching Junior and his father, Lucy kept her head down staring at her feet.

"Hello Reverend John," said Lucy, as she reached the shade and sank down on the soft grass.

Reverend John was shocked when he saw Lucy. She had seemed so young and beautiful, so full of life the day he married her and Junior. This girl sitting before him now was a shell of her former self. How could this have happened in such a short period of time? He turned to Junior with a withering look.

"Get her some water Junior, and I want to hear from her if she wants to be out here," said Reverend John.

"Oh, she does Daddy. Don't you Lucy?" said Junior, as he handed Lucy the water jug, digging his finger nails into her hand as he did so.

Lucy knew this was a warning from Junior to do as he had told her. "Yes Reverend John, I want to be here with Junior," Lucy said, barely able to get the words out.

"How are things going with you two?" asked Reverend John.

"We are doing great, Daddy," said Junior, before Lucy could answer.

"I want to hear from Lucy," said Reverend John, glaring at his son.

"That's right, we are doing all right," said Lucy, seeing the warning look in Junior's eyes.

Reverend John suspected that all was not well with Junior and Lucy but did not have the heart to press further. After all, if the girl herself said everything was fine, then he guessed it was so. Still he felt obligated to remind Junior that Lucy was his wife and help mate and he should treat her kindly. With that done, he got up and left, happy to be on his way. Now he could tell Ms. Alva he had talked to Junior and hoped that would be the end of the matter.

Weeks drug by and life went on as usual for Lucy. Junior treated her a little better after the talk with his father. At least he was careful where he hit her. He made sure he did not leave a mark where it could be seen. Thankfully for Lucy, the harvesting season had passed and work had started on the promised house. At this point, Lucy had no interest in the house or even the next day for that matter. She simply existed. Junior made sure she never had an opportunity to leave by nailing the door shut if he left without her. He would attend church occasionally to keep his father pacified but never took Lucy with him for fear she would talk to her Granny Alva. He made excuses to his father about why Lucy could not attend.

After numerous trips by the cabin, only to find no one home, Granny Alva had given up on finding Lucy alone. She could only pray her Granddaughter was well. She was not in the best of health and had Lucy's sisters to care for. They were thriving under her care and were a blessing to her as well. They had quit asking questions about why they no longer saw Lucy. The young are resilient. They loved their sister but knew nothing of her plight, therefore, went about their own lives. Granny Alva felt no need to burden them with it as they could do nothing to help.

CHAPTER 12

As the days went by, Lucy began to accept her fate and gave up the idea of leaving Junior. As he saw the change, he slowly relaxed his vigil over her. It was beginning to wear on him as well. His obsession was depriving him of his freedom as much as Lucy. They had started work on the new house and he hated having Lucy moping about all the time. He was no longer free to visit the Turney Sisters as he had planned. Since marrying Lucy, he seemed to have no fun at all, he pouted. Lucy was weary of coming to the building site as well. She wasn't allowed any input into the construction and other than preparing lunch for the family members, just seemed to be in the way.

One morning as Lucy was preparing their breakfast, she suddenly felt quite ill. The smell of the fatback she was frying sent her flying to the back door. She barley made it through the door when she threw up all over the steps.

"What's wrong with you this morning? We have to get a move on. Daddy will have my hide if we are late again," said Junior, showing little sympathy.

"Please Junior, I am not feeling well this morning. Can't I stay here this morning and bring lunch over later?" asked Lucy weakly.

She knew she would have to walk the distance to the new house carrying the lunch pail but did not care at the moment. She did not understand what had come over her all of a sudden. She had felt fine when she went to bed last night.

Junior debated on leaving Lucy behind but felt reasonably safe in doing so. Ms. Alva seemed to have given up on her quest to get Lucy away from him. She still asked about her on the occasions he saw her at church. She always asked the same thing. "Where is Lucy? Why is she not here with you?" Of course he always told her she was fine but needed a day of rest with all she had to do.

Ms. Alva never knew when Junior was going to be at church. She had purposefully stayed at home several times and had Thomas take her by the cabin but could never get anyone to the door. She had no way of knowing Junior had told Lucy he would kill her sisters and Granny Alva if she left him. Truthfully, Junior would have never had the nerve to do such a thing. As is the way with most people like Junior, they are cowards at heart. After being told this numerous times, however, Lucy grew to believe him.

After considering for a moment, Junior agreed to let Lucy stay home with a warning to be there with their lunch at noon sharp. It might be nice to have a pot of warm soup for a change instead of the cold biscuits and such they had been taking with them. With that Junior left, slamming the door behind him.

Lucy sat in the rocker for awhile trying to get her stomach to settle. She got up and made a tea with some herbs as her grandmother had taught her. This seemed to help some. She had no time to dawdle, however. There were so many things she had let go around the cabin. She had lunch to prepare and laundry to do.

Lucy had the soup simmering on the stove and was feeling considerably better when she noticed the water bucket was almost empty. She grabbed the bucket and had just started down the path to the spring when she saw Uncle Thomas' old truck pull up outside the cabin. He had hardly pulled the truck to a halt when Granny Alva climbed out the door, moving faster than Lucy had seen her in a long time. They rushed toward each other, with tears streaming down their faces.

"Oh Lucy, at last, at last," cried Granny Alva, reluctant to let her Granddaughter go.

"I know Granny," cried Lucy. "I have missed you all so much."

They made their way back to the cabin where Lucy said hello to her Uncle and they settled themselves down to chat.

Granny Alva noticed how thin Lucy was. The light seemed to have gone from her eyes. It broke her heart to see Lucy this way.

"The girls will be so excited to hear we have talked," said Granny Alva. "Marcy is seeing George Willis from over in the next county." They seem to be getting serious and I suspect there will be plans for a wedding soon."

"That's wonderful Granny. Is he a nice boy? Does he treat Marcy well?" asked Lucy anxiously.

Granny Alva knew the reason for Lucy's questions and assured her that George was a nice boy.

"Lucy, you do not look well. Thomas and I tried so many times to see you but you were never home. We have been worried sick about you," said Granny Alva.

Her Grandmother's concern brought tears to Lucy's eyes. It had been so long since she had heard a kind word.

"I know you did Granny, but Junior made me go everywhere with him. I have been very tired lately and this morning the strangest thing happened. I felt perfectly fine, then all of a sudden, as I was fixing breakfast, I got really sick to the point of throwing up."

Granny Alva and Thomas looked at each other. The situation had suddenly gotten worse. This poor child was probably pregnant and did not know it. It would be even harder now to get her away from Junior.

"Lucy, I suspect you may have a little one on the way. I want you to pack your things this instant while we have the chance. We will manage somehow even with a baby. I can tell you are not happy here and I suspect things have not changed with Junior," said Granny Alva, rising from her chair.

Lucy felt stunned at what her Granny told her. Could it be true? She was going to have a baby? She knew there was no way Junior would ever let her leave, even more so now. This was the way with Junior's family. They wanted big families with lots of children to help out with the farm work. She knew she was trapped now for all time. Just as she had known when her mother died, she was committed to this life just as she had been then. The only difference was, this was a commitment for life.

With resignation in her voice, Lucy rose from her chair and took her Grandmother's hand. "I know you love me Granny and I appreciate more than you can ever imagine your concern. I can't leave now if I am pregnant. You know Junior would never allow it. This baby will be a blessing to me. I will have someone to love and it will love me in return. Strangely, I feel at peace. My life is set out for me now, and I will be fine."

"Lucy, I beg you to reconsider. You don't have to live this way. We will manage somehow," Granny Alva pleaded.

Seeing Lucy's resolve, Thomas stepped in and asked Lucy if there was anything she needed before they left.

"Why yes there is Uncle Thomas. I have to take this pot of soup over to Junior and his family for their lunch. It would be a great help to me if you could drop me off there. I was dreading the walk."

"Lucy, please reconsider," said Granny Alva. Now that this opportunity had come, she could not believe she would have to leave her Granddaughter behind.

Lucy kissed her Grandmother on the cheek and tried to reassure her she would be fine. "Now that I am pregnant, I have a feeling Junior will be a lot better to me as children are important to his family and he wants to please his father."

"All right Lucy. If that is what you want, but I intend to have a word with that young man when we take you to deliver that soup," said Granny Alva.

Alarmed, Lucy pleaded with her Grandmother to be nice when speaking to Junior. "I will need lot's of advise with this baby Granny and I want you and the girls to be a part of our lives. Maybe if Junior sees you have accepted our situation, he will let me see you occasionally."

Junior could not believe what he was seeing when Thomas' truck pulled up and Lucy got out. Thomas helped his mother out of the truck and took the pot of soup from Lucy. Junior stiffened his spine as they approached him. He knew he had to be careful as his father was standing nearby.

"Hello Junior," Granny Alva said accusingly. "Lucy asked us to give her a lift to deliver your lunch. We were happy to do so, considering the walk she would have had otherwise."

Junior only nodded his head, glaring at Lucy. He was not quite sure what to expect. He saw his father approaching and decided to be cordial for now and see how things went.

"Ms. Alva, Thomas, how you folks doing?" asked Reverend John, a bit uneasy himself. He had not spoken to Ms Alva since her visit at his home several weeks before when she accused his son of mistreating Lucy.

"Oh, we are doing OK, considering," said Ms. Alva. I see the house is coming along." Ms Alva was not that impressed, however. She could see it was not going to be what she had hoped for Lucy. It would be a little larger than the cabin but was still only two rooms with a small front porch.

"You may want to add another room since our Lucy appears to be in the family way."

The words were out before Granny Alva realized what she was saying. She knew she should have let Lucy take care of this announcement. Still, she wanted to be sure she could be a part of Lucy's life from now on.

If she could assure Junior she had no intentions of taking Lucy away from him, maybe that could happen.

Junior stared from Lucy to her Grandmother. He wasn't sure if this was good news or bad news. He could hardly see himself as a father. Still, when he saw the proud look on his father's face, he felt a sense of accomplishment. At last, he had done something to make his father proud. He gave Lucy and the baby no thought in the matter.

"Why that is wonderful news, Lucy," said Reverend John, patting her awkwardly on the back. Turning to the rest of the family, Reverend John called out, "Junior is going to be a daddy."

There was much whooping and slapping Junior on the back. Lucy was surprised at the excitement but pleased as well. At this moment she truly felt a part of this family. Granny Alva stood with her arm around Lucy's shoulders. She was pleased with the reception of Lucy's news.

Everyone gathered round to enjoy the soup Lucy had brought and there was lots of kidding and joking among the brothers. When the meal was over, Lucy was not sure if she would be required to stay. She need not have worried however, Reverend John made that decision.

"Ms. Alva, Thomas, would you mind dropping Lucy off back at the cabin? We have to take special care of her now that she is in the family way. Ms. Alva, I know

Lucy will need you around a lot and I am sure you will be more than happy to help her if needed," said Reverend John, giving Junior a hard look. "Allie will be so excited to hear the news," he said, as Thomas helped Lucy and Ms. Alva into the truck.

"I will see you tonight Junior," said Lucy, as the truck pulled away. She did not know why she felt the need to reassure him but this was a new start and she would do her part in making it work.

Granny Alva and Thomas dropped Lucy off with strict instructions from her Granny to take care of herself. "I will be back in a few days and we will go over all the things you are going to need," said Granny Alva. Lucy's sisters would be so excited to hear news of Lucy and would be thrilled at the idea of visiting her.

CHAPTER 13

Everything changed for Lucy. No longer did Junior require her to go everywhere with him. Granny Alva and Lucy's sisters visited often bringing with them things Lucy would need for the coming baby. The morning sickness had passed and Lucy began to look her old self. She was able to do all her chores and have dinner ready for Junior when he came home at night. He still wasn't particularly nice to Lucy but rather enjoyed having his bath ready and his meals on the table when he arrived home. The new house was coming along nicely and would be ready in another month. He no longer found Lucy that attractive, now that she was pregnant. He found the Turney Sisters much more exciting and went to visit them often. Lucy thought this might be normal behavior and did not question his sudden loss of desire for her. Truthfully, she was glad she did not have to suffer through Junior's crude lovemaking anymore. She focused on the coming baby and her love for the life growing inside her was all she needed.

Ms. Allie had come around and seemed to have forgiven Ms. Alva for the criticism of her precious

Junior. As Lucy's time drew near, there were heated discussions as to who would act as midwife. Granny Alva felt it should be her since she was Lucy's actual Grandmother. Ms. Allie argued she had delivered all her Grandchildren and felt this one should be no exception. The dispute was settled by Lucy who told them she wanted them both there assisting her. They grudgingly agreed.

It was a bright sunny day when Lucy's pains started. At the instruction of his father, Junior had been staying closer to home in expectation of the birth. Lucy woke him as the sun rose and asked him to fetch Ms. Alva and his Mother. Junior got out of bed and dressed, grumbling that the baby had interrupted his sleep on his first day of rest in a while.

They had moved into the new house two months earlier. Lucy had the new cradle her Uncle Thomas had made for her stationed by the bed. The tiny baby clothes Ms. Alva and her sisters had made were folded neatly and tucked away. Ms. Alva had given Lucy her first dresser when she had moved into the new house. It was Lucy's most prized possession.

At exactly two O'clock that afternoon, Lucy's baby was born. The sun's rays shown through the window and seemed to pool around they tiny bundle as he was placed into her arms. She decided that instant to name him Sunny.

The days slipped by and Lucy was happier than she had been in years. Sunny was a toddler now and was the joy of everyone's life. Everyone's except Junior, it seemed. He paid little attention to Sunny except when the little boy did something he disapproved of. When his father was around, however, Junior appeared to be the most devoted of fathers. Lucy worried about Junior's temper and tried to keep Sunny out of his way. She had come to know of Junior's cruelty all too well and she swore it would never be directed at her son.

Granny Alva did not visit as often now. She was getting more fragile and Lucy feared she would not have her much longer. Greta and Marcy were both married now so Granny Alva was alone again. Greta and her new husband had moved into Lucy's old cabin until they could do better. Since Greta lived closer than Lucy or Marcy, it went without question that she would check in on their Grandmother whenever possible as well as did Thomas.

Spring had come again and everything was coming to life. Lucy loved this time of year. After her chores were done, she and Sunny would take strolls along the creek bank. Lucy would point out the different plants and trees, naming them for Sunny just as Granny Alva had done for her. Occasionally Sunny would spy a frog and dash into the shallow creek to catch it before Lucy could stop him.

Junior was busy with his brothers doing the spring planting. Even though Lucy stayed busy at home, Junior seemed to resent the fact that Lucy no longer worked in the fields. He started coming home in the foulest of moods. At least once a week now, he came home, bathed in the bath Lucy prepared for him and left. There was never a word to Lucy as to where he was going or when he would be back. Some times he would be gone all night. Lucy never questioned him as she really did not care. She knew she would never have a loving marriage and directed all her love to Sunny and his care.

Junior failed to find Lucy attractive now even though she was actually more beautiful than ever. He did take her occasionally if he was upset about something and was brutal in doing so. There was also the occasional fist to the stomach or kidney just to let her know he was still boss.

Lucy tolerated this mistreatment without a word. She could take the punishment as long as he left Sunny alone. That hope was short lived, however. They were eating breakfast one morning and little Sunny knocked over Junior's coffee cup. The hot liquid ran into Junior's lap before he could move. The lick was so quick Lucy could do nothing to stop it. Little Sunny lay in a heap on the floor sobbing. Lucy was so enraged she could hardly move. She grabbed Sunny from the floor, checking him for injuries. The side of his little face and ear were red and already swelling from the blow.

"How could you do such a thing?" Lucy screamed at Junior. "He is only a baby. You're a monster to do such a thing."

Lucy had never raised her voice to Junior and for a
moment he was motionless. He stared at Lucy and
slowly the rage overpowered him. He struck Lucy in
the face with his fist sending her sprawling backwards.
Luckily, she was standing near the bed which broke
her fall. She still held onto Sunny and tried to clear
her head. The blow had left her stunned but she knew
she had to protect Sunny at all costs.

"I'm sorry Junior. I don't know what came over me,"
Lucy whispered, hoping this would calm him.

"You damn well better be sorry and you had better
keep that brat away from me from now on," said
Junior, and gave Lucy another slap across the face for
good measure.

Lucy and Sunny were both sobbing now and this
seemed to please Junior. He showed her, he thought.
Bet she would remember this for awhile and keep her
mouth shut. He was the man of the house and would
discipline his son how and when he chose.

With that, Junior left the house for the fields. Lucy
lay with Sunny in her arms, crying until she could cry
no more. She noticed little Sunny had stopped crying
also and had dropped off to sleep, his thumb in his
mouth. Lucy noticed he had started this habit when
Junior scolded him about something. She put a light
blanket over Sunny and slowly rose from the bed. She
went to the dresser and was shocked by the look of
her face. Her right eye was already starting to turn
blue and swell. The slap had burst her lower lip and

blood trickled down her chin. She stood looking at herself in the mirror and made a decision. She would take Sunny and go to Granny's today while Junior was gone. She had to get Sunny away from here.

Lucy packed as much of her belongings as she could carry. She knew she would have to carry Sunny most of the way as his little legs could not carry him far. She took a flour sack and stuffed it with all Sunny's things. She hated to leave the things Granny Alva had given her but knew her Grandmother would understand. With the sack slung across her shoulder with a make shift strap, she picked little Sunny up, still sleeping and walked out the door.

It was slow going, as Lucy had to stop and rest every once in awhile. Sunny had awakened by now and was excited when Lucy explained they were going to visit Granny Alva. He loved his Great Grandmother just as Lucy and her sister's had. Once Lucy heard a car approaching but hid in the bushes for fear it might be someone in Junior's family. She watched the car pass by and continued down the road. She knew there was no need to try and hide her tracks as Junior would know exactly where she had gone. She had no place else to go.

She was totally exhausted by the time she reached her Grandmother's house. Little Sunny was becoming weary of the journey also and was starting to get cranky. Granny Alva took one look at Lucy and with a gasp pulled her and Sunny into her arms.

"My God, what has he done to you?"

Lucy sank to the floor still holding Sunny in her arms. Granny Alva pulled up her chair and took little Sunny on her lap. She sat slowly rocking, stroking Lucy's hair. She was so angry that God let things like this happen to good people. And little Sunny, just a baby who could not harm a soul.

They sat there in silent misery for awhile. Lucy's strength began to return and she knew she had to take care of Sunny. He was probably thirsty after their long walk.

"Granny, I can't live there any more. I am afraid of what will happen to Sunny if I stay. I know Junior will be here causing trouble and I hate to ask you but I don't have any where else to go. Greta and Marcy don't have room and they don't need the extra burden," Lucy said, feeling ashamed to ask this of her Grandmother.

"There will be no more discussion about it," said Granny Alva. "You will stay here and we can handle that Junior if he comes around here. I still have my shotgun. You will have to stay close to the house I am afraid, at least for awhile. Maybe if he sees you mean business it won't take him long to give up and leave you be."

Granny settled Lucy and Sunny in the girl's old bedroom and fixed them some lunch. Neither of them had much appetite. They sat in dreaded silence most of the afternoon waiting for what they knew was coming.

The sun was just setting when they heard the sound of an approaching vehicle. It came to a screeching halt just outside Granny Alva's door, a cloud of dust behind it. Granny Alva rose and reached for her shotgun which she had loaded earlier.

"I know you are in there, now get out here this minute," screamed Junior, sounding almost hoarse with rage.

Granny Alva moved closer to the door. She and Lucy had barred the door earlier by blocking it with a chest of drawers. A chair had been placed under the door knob of the back door as well as bolted. They had closed and bolted the shutters in expectation of Junior's arrival. The only light in the house was provided by a lamp sitting on the kitchen table. Lucy sat in a corner with Sunny, too petrified with fear to move. Her eye was almost swollen shut now and she looked like a cornered animal. The sight of her made Granny Alva even more determined.

"You go away, Junior. After what you did to Lucy and this baby of yours, you deserve to be hung. They will never set foot in your house again as long as I have a breath left in my body," Granny Alva yelled, gasping for breath.

"That may not be long if you don't open this door, you crazy old hag," screamed Junior as he began to kick on the door.

"What do you mean, after what you did to Lucy and this baby?" came another voice from outside the door.

Granny Alva recognized the voice as that of Reverend John and felt a small sense of relief.

"He beat them both this morning over nothing. Lucy can hardly see from the black eye he gave her and little Sunny's face is still swollen and red. They will be staying with me from now on," Granny Alva called, hoping the Reverend could reason with his son.

Reverend John stood motionless, as if in deep thought. He looked at Junior who stood twisting his hands.

"How do I know what you say is true?" asked Reverend John.

"Oh it's true," said Granny Alva.

Reverend John wavered in indecision. "Is what she says true Junior?"

"I barley touched them Daddy. Besides, they deserved what ever I gave them," said Junior, sullenly.

"Open the shutter and let me see their faces," said Reverend John.

"Do I have your word you won't try to enter the house if I do?" Granny Alva responded.

"You have it."

Granny Alva turned to Lucy and motioned for her to come to the window. Lucy rose and came to stand behind Granny Alva, still holding Sunny in her arms. Granny Alva opened the shutters wide enough for the Reverend to get a good look at Lucy and Sunny. Lucy's eye was completely shut now. Little Sunny, seeing Junior, began to cry and turned his face into Lucy's neck but not before Reverend John got a good look at him.

There was an audible gasp from Reverend John as he saw what his son had done. He had never felt such rage. Before he could get control of his anger, Junior's father turned and struck his son full across the face. Junior staggered backwards from the unexpected blow, landing on his backside in the dirt. He sat dazed for a moment. His father had never struck him before and he was not quite sure what to do. As his senses returned, Junior felt the anger rising in him. He rose, and took a step towards his father, fists clinched.

"I wouldn't advise that Junior," said Reverend John, standing his ground.

Junior stood uncertainly for a moment then stomped away. He could always come back later without his father. He would not let this old woman get the best of him.

"I am sorry Lucy for Junior's behavior. I am afraid his mother and I have spoiled him. I promise you, if you go back home, Junior will never strike you again," said Reverend John.

Granny Alva turned to look at Lucy who had retreated to her corner, trying to comfort little Sunny.

"I don't think Lucy will be returning to Junior, Reverend. He has never been a decent husband to Lucy and I will not have her near him another day. I know he is your son and it's hard to see our children's faults. Some people are just born bad and I think Junior is one of those people. Lucy will be staying with me," said Granny Alva, closing the shutter as an indication the conversation was over.

Feeling he had no choice at the moment, Reverend John, turned to leave.

"I hope you all will reconsider. Sleep on it and I will be back tomorrow to check on the welfare of my Grandson." With that parting remark, Reverend John made his way back into the truck where a sullen Junior sat waiting.

Granny Alva let out a slow breath, feeling all the energy drain from her. She had stood her ground and won for the moment but she felt the fight wasn't over. She hoped she would be strong enough to see Lucy through this.

Feeling totally exhausted, Granny Alva suggested they retire early that night. They ate a light supper and bathed Little Sunny who fell asleep immediately afterwards. Granny Alva shared the bed with Lucy and Sunny. Even though cramped, there seemed to be some comfort for them in the closeness. As Granny

Alva lay listening to their breathing, she felt the familiar pangs of pain in her chest. They were becoming more frequent now and she feared what was coming, for Lucy's sake.

"Lord, keep me here long enough to see Lucy through this," she prayed.

Granny Alva awakened as the first beams of sunlight cast its rays through the slits in the shuttered windows. She felt a little better even though they had all tossed about in restlessness throughout the night. She dressed and made her way into the spare bedroom to use the chamber pot. Normally she would have made the walk out back to the out house but the doors were still blocked. She hoped they would be able to move the barriers today. Maybe Junior would have come to his senses and leave Lucy alone.

That hope was short lived, however. As they sat eating their breakfast, they heard a vehicle come to a halt outside the house. Lucy looked across the table at her Grandmother with a look of pure fear. She instinctively rose and made her way to the bed where Sunny still slept.

Granny Alva reached for the shotgun which she had placed near the door. She peeked through the shuttered window and drew in her breath when she saw Junior. He was in his brother's truck and he was alone. This was bad, Granny Alva thought. His father was not there to keep him in check. There was no telling what Junior would do.

"Lucy, I want you out here with my son this minute," Junior yelled. "I will break down the door if I have to."

Lucy came to stand behind her Grandmother, not quite sure what to do. Granny Alva stood in indecision herself, trying to decide what action to take.

"Lucy, I will give you three minutes to open that door and get yourself out here. You are coming home with me one way or another. If you come out willingly, no one will get hurt," said Junior.

"What can we do Granny? I am afraid of what he is going to do. I don't want you or Sunny to get hurt. Maybe I should just take Sunny and go with him," said Lucy, her shoulders slumping in defeat.

"You'll do no such thing," Granny Alva whispered.

"Go away Junior. Lucy and Sunny are staying with me and that's the end of it."

Hearing this, Junior's rage overcame him. He began kicking the door, ranting at Lucy and her Grandmother as he did so. Seeing that he would not be able to enter the house that way, he began tugging on the shutters that covered the windows. They were quite old and came off without much effort from Junior.

Granny Alva and Lucy backed away from the window as Junior's red face appeared. They knew he was not going to stop at this point. Granny Alva raised the shotgun and pointed it above Junior's head, hoping that would discourage him.

"You think that scares me old woman," Junior screamed. "I know you won't use that gun. Now open the door or I am smashing this window, makes no difference to me."

"I am telling you Junior, get away from here. You know your father would not want you here acting like this," Granny Alva said, hoping the mention of his father would bring him to his senses.

This only seemed to enrage Junior more. He raised the end of his gun and smashed the window. Just as he reached in to unlatch the window, Granny Alva fired the shotgun. The gun's recoil knocked her to the floor on her back. The shot went over Junior's head, blowing a hole in the wall above the window.

Seeing Granny Alva on the floor and the shotgun lying out of her reach, Junior raised the window and climbed over the sill into the room.

The shot had awakened Little Sunny and he was crying at the top of his lungs. The sound of Sunny's crying brought Lucy out of her shock and she ran to pick him up. Cradling him in her arms she ran and sank to the floor by Granny Alva who was trying to upright herself.

"Get your things and let's go," said Junior, as he slid the chest away from the door.

A strange calm came over Lucy as she watched her Grandmother struggling on the floor. Her breath was coming in short gasps and she was very pale. This brave, fragile woman had stood so strong in trying to protect her and Sunny. Maybe it was time she stood up for herself. She helped her Grandmother to the nearby rocker, placed the still sobbing Sunny in her lap and turned to Junior.

"Sunny and I will not be going with you Junior. You are not a good husband nor are you a good father. Abusing me was one thing but I will not have Sunny mistreated by you or anyone else. You can see Sunny as often as you like here at Granny's house. Now please go and leave us in peace."

Junior stood uncertainly for a moment. He had never seen this Lucy before and was not quite sure what to do for a moment. He looked from Lucy to her Grandmother and seeing the most important thing in the world to Lucy, grabbed little Sunny and turned to the door.

Lucy froze in fear. Not Sunny, not her baby. She would not let him take Sunny. She would die first. Before she could think about what she was doing, she lunged for the shotgun on the floor. She had never fired a gun before or she would have known the gun was no longer loaded. The shots were lodged in the wall above Granny Alva's window.

Junior did know, however, and laughed as Lucy pointed the gun at him. He approached her with a look of pure evil and while holding Little Sunny in one arm, slapped Lucy hard across the face. Still laughing, he walked out the door, taking with him the thing that meant most to Lucy.

Lucy started for the door but heard a sound behind her. She turned to look back as she reached the door. Her Grandmother sat on the edge of the rocker, her arms outstretched to Lucy. Torn, Lucy turned back to follow Junior but stopped when she glanced her Grandmother toppling to the floor.

"Granny," Lucy screamed. Kneeling by her Grandmother, Lucy could see she was having trouble breathing. She was trying to say something but Lucy could not make out the words. They were barely a whisper so Lucy had to lean near her Grandmother's face to hear.

"Thomas, go see Thomas," her Grandmother whispered. "I love …."

Lucy knew her Grandmother was gone. She had never felt such devastation and the thought flittered through her mind to end it all herself. She felt more was being asked of her than she could bear. Her baby was being taken away and her Grandmother, the one rock in her life, was now gone. She sat sobbing, and finally lay down beside her Grandmother, cradling herself near the body.

Around noon, Thomas came by his mother's for his usual visit. He tried to check in on her every other day. She was alone now and getting quite old. He was alarmed when he saw the broken window. Of course he did not know of the previous day's events. Thomas called out for his mother as he reached the porch steps. Hearing no response, Thomas entered the door in alarm. What he saw was worse than he feared. His mother was lying lifeless on the floor with Lucy still snuggled next to her, sound asleep. Her arm was now placed across her Grandmother's body and for a moment, Thomas thought they were both dead. Taking his Mother's pulse, Thomas confirmed she was gone. Seeing Lucy's shallow breathing, Thomas gently shook her awake.

"Lucy honey, Lucy, wake up."

Lucy could hear her Uncle but did not want to wake up. Somewhere in the back of her mind she knew it was better to stay asleep. The pain would be too great. She would just stay asleep, she thought. Thomas shook her harder now and spoke more firmly. "Lucy, wake up. I need your help, wake up."

Slowly Lucy opened her eyes. Feeling her Grandmother's body next to her, it all came rushing back.

"They're all gone now Uncle Thomas," Lucy whispered. "Granny, my Little Sunny, I'm tired now Uncle Thomas. Just let me sleep."

"Lucy, what happened here? Where is Sunny? What do you mean he's gone?" Thomas asked, getting more alarmed by the minute. Looking closer at Lucy, he noticed her black eye and the swollen lip. "What happened, Lucy?" he asked gently, his heart breaking.

"Junior hurt Sunny so I came to Granny's. He showed up here this morning. Granny tried to protect us and look what happened to her Uncle Thomas. It is my fault. I should never have brought my problems here." Lucy was sitting now. The tears were streaming down her face but she made no sound at all.

"Did Junior do something to Mama?" Thomas asked, confused as to just what happened.

After hearing the rest of the story, Thomas knew the stress of the mornings events had probably brought on a heart attack. He knew of his mother's heart condition but kept it from everyone as his mother had asked him to. She explained she did not want people "tiptoeing" around her as if she were on her death bed.

Thomas helped Lucy to her feet and led her to his mother's rocker. Her face was swollen from all the crying and the right eye was almost shut from Junior's blow.

"Lucy, where is Sunny?" Thomas asked, trying to stay calm.

This brought a loud wail from Lucy and the tears started afresh.

"Junior took him Uncle Thomas. He took my baby. When I wouldn't go with him he grabbed Sunny and left," Lucy sobbed.

Thomas took Lucy in his arms and held her until the sobbing stopped.

"Lucy, we have to take care of Mama. We will get Sunny back and we will do it today, but right now, we have to take care of Mama and I need your help," said Thomas, hoping his appeal for help would bring Lucy out of her despair. If he could have gotten his hands on Junior at this moment, he felt he might truly have killed him.

Sighing, Lucy looked at her Uncle. "All right Uncle Thomas. Tell me what you want me to do."

Standing, Thomas took his mother's body and placed it on the bed, covering her with a sheet. He did not want to leave his mother alone but knew he could not leave Lucy here in her fragile condition. He had to make a decision between the living and the dead. He would have to take Lucy with him. He had to think. Normally when someone died, Reverend John was one of the first people notified. Thomas did not feel right about being around Reverend John and his family at this time but knew if Lucy had any chance of getting her son back, it would be through Reverend John.

"Lucy, honey, I know this will be a hard thing to do but we have to go see Reverend John. You know he is the only one who seems to have any control over

Junior. If we are to get Little Sunny back, that is our best approach."

Lucy cringed at the thought of seeing Junior's family. She did not know if she had the strength but knew her Uncle was right.

"I understand, Uncle Thomas. What about Granny?" said Lucy, starting to tear up again as she glanced at her Grandmother.

"Your Grandmother is in a much better place, Lucy. You know she would want you to get Little Sunny back. We will close the door and return as quickly as possible," said Thomas. He knew he had to keep Lucy focused or she could slip back into the black hole she seemed to be in when he found her.

"All right, let's get in the truck and go for help. Your Aunt Dottie will want to know what's going on. We will stop by there on our way to Reverend John's. We will need her help later and she can be getting ready while we go on."

Reverend John was just stepping upon his porch with his arms full of fire wood when Lucy and her uncle pulled up in front of the house. He dropped the wood where he stood when he saw Lucy.

"In heavens name Lucy, what ever is the matter? Where is Sunny?" asked Reverend John, real concern in his voice.

Lucy opened her mouth to answer but nothing came out. The tears started again and Thomas led her back to the truck. Reverend John followed, beginning to feel some real unease as he feared this might have something to do with Junior.

Thomas turned to Reverend John and spoke in a tight controlled voice. "Junior came to Mama's this morning demanding Lucy and Little Sunny return with him. When Lucy refused, he forced his way into the house. There was an altercation and I am sorry to say Mama is dead."

Reverend John staggered backwards as if he had been struck. "Oh no, please God, don't tell me Junior killed Ms. Alva," Reverend John said, in a broken, pleading voice.

"Mama has had a heart condition for some time. She didn't want people to know. I fear the stress brought on by Junior's visit may have brought on an attack. I had no choice but to leave her there alone. I went by for my normal visit with Mama this morning and found her lying on the floor. Lucy was curled up asleep next to her Grandmother. For a moment I feared she was gone too. She is in a very fragile condition and I am afraid if we don't get Sunny back to her soon she may have a mental collapse. You know that child means everything to her."

Reverend John looked as if he was aging before their eyes. He was a tall man who usually stood tall and erect. That pride seemed to have been taken away from him in a matter of minutes. He now stood pale and slumped, as though he was having trouble keeping himself upright.

"I am sorry for your loss Thomas," Reverend John said, trying to bring some sanity back into the morning. "I am also sorry for the actions of my son. I thought I had convinced him to wait and give Lucy time to reconsider. I should never have trusted that he would do the right thing. I am afraid I have to accept that Junior is not all that I hoped he would be. If you think Lucy is up to it, we will go get Little Sunny now."

Lucy had been sitting in the truck, resting her head on the back of the seat. Hearing this, she raised her head and whispered, "My son is all I have now Reverend. Please do what you can to help me."

Thomas pulled the truck up in front of Junior and Lucy's house. They all sat for a moment, as if bracing for what was to come. Reverend John sighed and said, "I guess we had best get this done. Lucy, please stay in the truck for now. I think Junior will be more responsive to handing Sunny over to me." Lucy could see Junior peering out the window. She did not see Sunny and prayed he was all right.

Reverend John approached the front steps and called to Junior as he did so. "Junior I want you out here with Little Sunny right now. You have caused enough harm for one day. Ms. Alva is dead and I am sorry to say, you may have played a part in her death. Open the door and hand little Sunny over to me."

"I didn't do anything to that old woman Daddy, she tried to shoot me. I bet they didn't tell you about that did they," said Junior, making no move towards the door.

"I know you didn't physically do anything to hurt Ms. Alva but your being there was the cause. Why didn't you do as I asked you to boy? I have seen what you did to Lucy and I don't blame her if she never comes back to this house. Now open this door and hand Little Sunny to me. We won't leave until you do."

Lucy heard Sunny crying and could stay in the truck no longer. She started for the house but her Uncle Thomas held her back. "Let Reverend John handle this for now Lucy."

Junior disappeared from the window and a moment later, pushed Sunny out the door. The little boy stumbled but Reverend John caught him before he toppled off the small porch. "I am ashamed to call you my son Junior," said Reverend John as he turned to hand Sunny to Lucy.

"He's my son too and you can't keep him from me," said Junior, as they turned to load back into the truck.

"We will talk about all of this later Junior. Right now we have to take care of Ms. Alva. If you make one move to bother Lucy or her family again until Lucy says it is all right, I will make you wish you were never born." Reverend John's tone was one that no one could ignore, not even Junior.

CHAPTER 14

It was decided that Dottie and Lucy would prepare the body for burial while the men built the burial box and dug the grave. Lucy brought out the beautiful flannel gown her Grandmother had made for her. It had never been worn and Lucy knew by now, it never would be. Dottie thought it a lovely gesture and the two women lovingly dressed the older woman who meant so much to them both.

Ms. Allie came by to pay her respects but did not stay long. She was cool and reserved. Lucy did not know if she was embarrassed about the actions of her son or if she blamed Lucy for all their problems. Lucy suspected the latter.

The church was overflowing the day of the funeral. Ms. Alva was known and loved by so many people. They all wanted to pay their respects. Reverend John did an especially fine job of preaching the funeral. Junior did not make an appearance and Lucy was grateful. After the funeral, Lucy and her family went back to Thomas' house. Food had been prepared for the family and anyone who might drop

by. It was well into the evening by the time all the
visitors left. It was just the family now, Lucy, Sunny,
Thomas, Dottie, Marcy and Greta with their husbands.
They sat around for awhile remembering special times
they had with Ms. Alva. Truth was everyone was avoiding the subject of Lucy and what her plans might be.

Finally Thomas decided to bring up the subject as
tactfully as he could. The past two days had been
horrendous for Lucy and Thomas knew she was near
collapse. He had just started to speak when Lucy
said, "Uncle Thomas I just remembered Granny's last
words to me. I could barely make the words out but
I think she said, "See Thomas" then she said "I love,"
then she was gone. Why do you suppose she said to
see you Uncle Thomas?"

"Well Lucy, I am glad you are all here so we can discuss
this together. Your Grandmother knew she didn't
have much time left. She talked to me a few months
ago about what she wanted done with her house and
belongings. She was most concerned about you Lucy.
She knew Junior did not treat you well and feared you
may need a place to stay someday. She knew Greta
and Marcy were both fortunate enough to find wonderful, reliable husbands and would be taken care
of. Your Grandmother wanted you to have this house
Lucy. There are a few personal items she wanted
Greta, Marcy and Dottie to have. She also had a small
amount of money she had saved over the years. There's
a small life insurance policy as well. She wanted that
divided four ways between you, the girls' and myself.

"Oh, I couldn't accept it Uncle Thomas. It is rightfully yours and Dottie's," Lucy stammered.

"Dottie and I have our own home which we built ourselves and it suits us nicely. I am sure Greta and Marcy would want you to have this house as well. You deserve it Lucy."

Lucy looked at her sister's who instantly rose and hugged her tight. "We have been so worried about you Lucy," said Marcy. "With this house, we'll have peace of mind knowing you'll always have a place to go, whether you stay with Junior or not."

"Then it's settled," said Thomas. "Our main concern however, is Lucy's present predicament. I think you need to stay here tonight Lucy, or one of you girl's should stay with her and Sunny, at least until we feel sure she is safe from Junior."

"Marcy and I will stay with her for a few days, Thomas," said Marcy's husband. "We've got old Rosco we'll bring over." Rosco was a great hunting dog but he was also very territorial. "If somebody comes snooping around in the night, he will eat the seat out of his pants."

Marcy and Joe stayed with Lucy for a week without incident. Lucy felt bad about keeping them from their own home. She knew there were things they needed to tend to so at the end of the week she told them they should return home. She had not seen or heard from Junior or Reverend John. She knew it was

just a matter of time. She could not hide here forever.
Lucy felt more at ease than she had in months. She
had a place of her own now for just her and Sunny. It
was a good house and she could make a good home
for Sunny here.

Two weeks had gone by and still no sign of Junior.
Lucy began to hope he had gone on to more exciting
things than her and Sunny. It was a beautiful sunny
day outside so Lucy told Sunny they would go on a
picnic for lunch. She had just finished preparing
their breakfast when she felt the first pangs of nausea.
This was the same way she had felt when she was pregnant with Sunny. Oh please God, don't let it be, she
prayed, but by noon she knew she was probably pregnant again.

Lucy had the little money her Granny had left her and
the house but she knew the money would not last forever. She would now have two children to cloth and
feed. What would she do when the money ran out?
She had to do some thinking.

It was Sunday afternoon when Lucy heard a vehicle
stop in front of the house. She peeped out the window
to see Reverend John approaching the house. He had
just recently learned to drive and was now getting himself about without one of his sons. Although Junior
was not with him, Lucy could not help but be fearful.

Revered John knocked on the door and Lucy knew
she had no choice but to open it and face what she
knew had been coming.

"Lucy, I trust you and Little Sunny are well," said Reverend John. "Could I come in and talk to you for a minute? I would like to see Sunny as well."

"Of course Reverend," said Lucy, opening the door.

Hearing his Grandfather, Sunny came running. He loved his Grandfather and Lucy knew he had missed seeing him.

"How's my big boy doing?" said Reverend John, lifting Sunny onto his lap.

"Me three now Paw Paw," said Sunny proudly. Lucy had been trying to teach him his numbers and how to spell his name. He was a bright little boy and seemed to flourish now that Junior wasn't around. He did not seem to miss his father at all.

"You are getting to be such a big boy Sunny. How about you take this peppermint stick now and run along and play while I talk to your mother," said Reverend John, sitting Sunny on the floor. Delighted with the candy, Sunny ran out to the porch swing Lucy had hung for him.

"Lucy, I have stayed away, and I made sure Junior stayed away, but I think it is time we talk about this situation. I know you have the house now and all but Little Sunny is Junior's son and I truly believe he misses him. I have had a long talk with him and I think if you can find it in your heart to forgive him, he will make you a good husband. In the eyes of God you are married until death. I know it is a hard thing to ask of you after what Junior did. If you will consider taking Junior back, I promise you he will never lay a hand on you or Sunny again."

"Reverend, I don't know that I can do what you ask. Junior has hurt me too deeply. It can never be erased, no matter what he does. I don't think I can take a chance on getting Little Sunny hurt again and now there is another baby on the way. How do you think Junior will feel about that Reverend? Junior hasn't exactly taken to fatherhood," said Lucy, with more conviction than she felt.

Reverend John looked shocked at this bit of news. "Then you have no choice Lucy. You can't possibly raise two children here alone. A new baby is wonderful news and I know Junior will be so proud. He has changed Lucy, and you will see if you just give him a chance," said Reverend John, almost pleading.

Lucy hated to hurt this old man's feelings. He did seem to have her interest at heart and she knew he truly loved Sunny. "I will think about it Reverend. Junior may come over and see Sunny if I have your assurance he will behave himself and leave when I tell him to."

"Oh, he will do that, I promise you," said Reverend John, almost jumping with joy. "I can't wait to tell Ellie the good news. Another baby on the way, she will be so pleased. She has missed seeing Little Sunny as much as I have. I tell you what, I will drive Junior over here tomorrow, drop him off, and pick him up an hour later, if that will relieve your mind."

"All right Reverend. We will see how it goes," said Lucy.

CHAPTER 15

And so the dance began, with Junior coming by for short periods of time, always on his best behavior. Even little Sunny had begun to relax around his father. Junior would come, spend a couple of hours at the end of the day and go home. Some times Lucy would invite him to stay and eat supper with her and Sunny. She felt little affection for Junior and knew now that she did not love him. However, as Reverend John had said, in the eyes of God, she was married to Junior for life. She knew she would never marry again whether she stayed with Junior or not.

Junior had never apologized to Lucy for his mistreatment. He just acted as though it had never happened. He never approached Lucy about sex or touched her in that way at all. Lucy did not know what she would have done if he had done so. She had no way of knowing Junior was just biding his time. He always had the Turney sisters to turn to for his sexual release, and he visited them quite often. He just knew he had to do whatever was necessary to get Lucy back. It was the only way he could get back in his father's good graces. He did not know why he was so obsessed with getting his father's approval. He saw the way people respected and looked up to his father. Somewhere deep inside, Junior wanted that same respect and admiration but knew he would probably always fall short.

Junior did not know how long he would have to play the good husband and father before Lucy agreed to take him back, but it did not matter that much. His mother fed him and did his laundry. He got his sex from the Turney sisters and went home to a peaceful house with no bawling kid around. Life wasn't so bad for Junior. He knew this could not go on indefinitely as his father was starting to press him about getting Lucy back home.

He had been doing some thinking and had decided he would approach Lucy about living in her Grandmother's house instead of the one they had built. It was a nicer house and larger. With this new baby coming they would need the room. It wasn't that far away from the fields so he didn't see why it wouldn't work.

The opportunity arose the very next day. Junior and Lucy were sitting in the porch swing watching Little Sunny play. It was a late summer evening and a cool breeze rustled the leaves of a nearby oak tree. Lucy sighed and closed her eyes for a moment. This was almost the way she had imagined her life would be. There was only one thing wrong, she did not love Junior and she was sure he did not love her.

Junior, sensing Lucy's mood, reached for her hand. Lucy tensed for a moment but relaxed as Junior gently closed his hand over hers.

"Lucy, I know you have reason to be concerned about coming back home but we can't go on like this forever," said Junior. "I have been doing some thinking. How would you feel about us patching things up and living right here in this house? That way you could kick me out if I don't do as you like," Junior said in a teasing tone. "This house is nicer than ours and with the new baby on the way, we will need the extra space. What do you think about that idea?"

Lucy sat for a moment, considering what Junior was proposing. "I will have to think about it Junior. You are right about one think for sure. I will not leave this house, for a lot of reasons. Mainly, I feel safe here. I will think about it and we will talk some more the next time you are here."

Junior knew he had to handle this carefully. He let go of Lucy's hand and stood to leave. "Give it serious thought Lucy and I will be back tomorrow evening. In the mean time, I will bring up the subject to Daddy. He will be excited about the prospect of us getting back together. I will have to talk to him about the house. I am sure he will understand if you want to stay here instead of the new house."

Junior said good night and ruffled Sunny's hair as he passed.

It was twilight now and still Lucy sat thinking about what Junior had said. Little Sunny ran around the yard chasing lightning bugs. He loved catching the bugs and gently placing them in a jar. As it grew dark, Sunny would watch the bugs in fascination as their tails would glow and then grow dim.

Lucy knew she did not want to return to things as they had been before. She had to feel comfortable Junior would not return to his old ways. Staying here in her Grandmother's house would give her some assurance in that. She would sleep on it and make her decision tomorrow, after her discussion with Junior.

Lucy called to Sunny to release his bugs and come into the house. The little boy was very careful not to hurt the bugs. This warmed Lucy's heart. She hoped he would always have this gentle nature.

The next morning, Junior talked to his father over the breakfast Ms. Allie had prepared. "Daddy, I think Lucy is ready to patch things up and start being my wife again. She insists on us living there in Ms. Alva's house though." Junior made it sound like this was Lucy's condition for their reconciliation, knowing his father would be more agreeable to the idea.

Reverend John was pleased to hear Lucy was willing to take Junior back. He was not quite sure how he felt about the house. He thought about it for a moment then said, "That's good news, Junior. Maybe that's not such a bad idea about the house. With the new baby coming you will need the extra room. Lottie and her new husband can move into your house when they get married.

Lottie was Junior's youngest sister who planned to marry the following month.

"Lottie's new husband works at the saw mill and won't be doing any farming. You will still own the land and continue to work it just as before," said Reverend John.

Junior assumed the subject was closed and rose to leave the table. To his surprise his father followed him outside.

"Junior, I didn't want to say anything in front of your mother, no need to upset her. You are very fortunate Lucy agreed to take you back after the way you treated her and Little Sunny." The way Junior had put it, his father assumed the decision had already been made. "I trust when you are together again there won't be a repeat of that kind of treatment," said Reverend John, with a warning tone that could not be missed.

"Oh no Daddy, things will be fine," Junior assured his father.

The next day after a long discussion with Junior, Lucy decided to take him back. He did seem to be a lot more mature now and she hoped he would become a good father to their children. She did give Junior a warning, however. "You will never strike Little Sunny, me or any of our children again," she had warned. To which Junior eagerly agreed. He would say whatever he had to for the moment, seething inside. How dare her threaten him, still he would do whatever necessary to get back in his father's good graces. There would be other ways to get his revenge on Lucy, in good time, he thought.

CHAPTER 16

Lucy's second child was born on a cold January night. She missed having her Grandmother in attendance. Ms. Allie was there but was still cool and aloof towards her. Lucy suspected she would never forgive her for leaving her precious son.

Baby Jesse was the complete opposite of Sunny. Where Sunny had red hair and blue eyes, Jesse had dark hair and brown eyes. Sunny was out going and into everything, Jesse was shy and quiet, preferring to entertain himself with the homemade toys Lucy gave him. She loved them both equally but had to admit, Sunny would always be special to her.

Since moving into the house, Junior had not attempted to make love to Lucy. She wondered about it sometimes but, truthfully, was relieved. He came and went, having little interaction with Lucy or the children. He was cordial enough but Lucy sensed an underlying current of anger. Sometimes she would catch Junior gritting his teeth if one of the children was cranky and acted up. She would sometimes discipline the children with a gentle swat on the seat. She could usually control them by just raising her voice.

During the winter months, the men busied themselves with hunting game, taking care of the farm animals and keeping their homes supplied with fire wood. Junior took care of these chores, although be it grudgingly. He still left the fetching of water to Lucy. Thankfully, Granny Alva had a well dug in the back yard so water was only a few steps away.

Junior kept his hunting gun propped in the corner of the living room. In those days, children grew up around guns and there never seemed to be any concern about safety.

One evening Sunny and Jesse were romping around the living room when one of them tripped over the gun. It hit the floor with a clatter. Junior jumped up inspecting the gun for damage. He discovered a scratch on the stock and pure fury overtook him. This gun was his prized possession, given to him on his tenth birthday by his father. He sat the gun in the corner, turned to the little boys who were now hiding behind Lucy, each clinging to a leg.

"I've had enough," said Junior, in a voice Lucy was all too familiar with. He took a step forward, his fists clinched at his side.

Lucy began to back away, pulling the children with her. "You will not touch these children Junior. They were just playing. Seeing Junior take another step forward,

Lucy said, "If you touch these children Junior, we are finished, for good this time."

Lucy saw the uncertainty cross Junior's face, and stood her ground. She would no longer cower before him and take his punishment. She had to be strong for her children's sake.

"I mean what I say Junior. This was our agreement and I will have it no other way."

Junior seethed with rage. He stood glaring at Lucy and the boys for a moment, then turned and stomped out of the house, slamming the door so hard the windows shook.

Lucy reassured the children as she bathed them and put them to bed with a bedtime story. They were all sound asleep when Junior returned. Lucy could smell the whisky on Junior's breath as he stumbled around in the dark. She hoped he would not wake the children. He tumbled into bed and was asleep in minutes. Sometime in the early morning hours, Lucy was awakened by Junior pawing at her gown. She tried to push him away but saw it was no use. If she put up too much a fight, they might wake the children. Junior took her savagely and brutally, whispering in her ear that he "was back" and "she had best take notice."

The next morning, Lucy rose before Junior. She knew the boy's would be getting up soon and would need caring for. Junior's clothes were strewn about the living room. Lucy gathered them up and tossed them on the floor beside the bed. She had to be strong this morning. She had to make Junior understand, she would not allow her children to be harmed. She supposed it was her wifely duty to be submissive to her husband. That was the thinking in Lucy's time. She could do that no matter how unpleasant, as long as he left her children alone.

Lucy fed the children and sent them out to play before Junior awakened. He walked into the kitchen just as Lucy finished with the breakfast dishes. He stood uncertainly for a second, then pulled out a chair and asked Lucy for coffee. Lucy poured the coffee and sat down across from Junior. "Junior, when we decided to get back together, you agreed to leave the discipline of the children to me. Since you can't seem to control your temper, it's the way it has to be. You need to understand that right now. I won't tolerate my children being mistreated. If you don't agree then you can leave right now."

There was no mention of last night, Junior noticed. All right, if that's the way she wanted it, then that's the way it would be. The bitch would pay every chance he got.

Days turned into weeks and Junior ignored the boy's for the most part but Lucy paid dearly when the sun went down. She spent her days in dread, feeling trapped. She knew she could not physically throw Junior out of the house. The only person who could control him was his father. How could she possibly explain to Reverend John that Junior was abusing her in the bedroom. With his biblical view, Lucy knew he would feel it was Lucy's duty to submit to her husband. Junior made sure he did not hit her or the boys. This was the one thing he knew his father would not approve of.

CHAPTER 17

The year's slipped by. There were more children now, two more boys and three little girls. The older boy's went to the fields now with their father. Lucy fought to keep the children in school during the school year. She was determined they would get an education, at what ever cost. Reverend John had died of pneumonia and the family seemed to have fallen apart. Junior and his brothers farmed half the land they had when their father was alive. They worked their children like farm animals. Junior and Lucy's agreement about disciplining the children had long gone by the wayside. Lucy tried her best to protect the boys but was helpless to do so. She had asked Junior to leave only to have him laugh at her. She had tried locking the doors to bar his entry into the house. He had only broken it down. Each time Lucy tried to get rid of Junior, she paid the price with a severe beating.

Marcy and Greta had moved away to the nearby city of Memphis. There was a war going on and their husband's were away in a foreign country. Marcy and Greta had gotten jobs in munitions factories in Memphis. Her Uncle Thomas had been hurt in a logging accident and had been unable to work since. She could not trouble them with her problems. Besides, Uncle Thomas had pleaded with Lucy not to take Junior back all those years before. Oh how she wished she had listened to him.

For some reason Lucy could not quite understand, Junior stayed away from the home brewed liquor his brother's seemed to enjoy so much. On the few times he had tried it, Junior found the drink made him feel totally out of control. On the last such venture it had gotten him a black eye and a broken rib brought on by a fight with his cousin, Maynard. The liquor seemed to enhance Junior's mean side and there was no reasoning with him. Maynard was quite a bit bigger than he was but Junior felt ten feet tall and twice as mean. The fight only lasted a few minutes and ended with Junior on his backside staring up at his laughing brothers. This infuriated Junior even more and he stomped away from the bunch of jeering men, his liquor bottle in hand.

By the time Junior reached home the bottle was empty. He could still hear his brothers laughing at him as the house came into view. Lucy was out in the yard fetching fire wood for the stove and Junior made a beeline for her. All the rage he felt surged to the surface. He was on Lucy before she knew what was happening. The load of wood she held in her arms tumbled to the ground as Junior grabbed her hair and jerked her near off her feet. Lucy screamed and tried to get away. She made it to the porch steps with Junior staggering after, cursing her all the way. Lucy could smell the whiskey on him and knew she was in trouble.

Hearing their mother's screams, the children came running out to see what was wrong. Sunny and Jesse were big boys but were so terrified of their father they were paralyzed to help. Junior struck Lucy full in the face with his fist, bringing a stream of blood out of her nose. The blood seemed to trigger the boys out of their fear and they both piled onto Junior's back trying with all their might to pull him off their mother. Junior had never felt such rage. He rose with both boys hanging on for dear life. Sunny was the first to hit the ground and received a kick to the head from Junior's boot. He lay still and Lucy feared he was dead.

Jesse was helpless now and gave up the struggle. Junior started hitting the helpless boy with his fists not caring where they landed. Lucy, fearing for her sons, knew she had to do something drastic. She picked up a stick of the wood she had been carrying and swung it at Junior's head. He looked up just in time to block the blow with his arm. He was on Lucy now, forgetting about the children. Lucy saw Sunny slowly sitting up and yelled for him to get the other children and run. The smaller children had been watching in horror, sobs racking their little bodies.

Sunny knew they could do nothing to help their mother so he did as she asked. He gathered the other children and Jesse, whose eyes were already swelling, and disappeared into the nearby woods. It would be dark soon and Sunny knew Junior would never find them. The children played in those woods and had many hiding places.

Seeing her children safely away, Lucy slipped down into the darkness. She wasn't sure if it was from the beating she was taking from Junior or just an escape from reality.

Hours later, Lucy heard voices from what seemed like a far away place. Sunny, it's the children, she thought. They must need me. She struggled to rouse herself as she felt a cool cloth being placed gently on her brow. It was still dark outside but as Lucy opened her eyes she could see the faces of her beloved children. Poor Jesse's eyes were only slits and this brought the reality back to her. She was lying on the front porch where Junior had left her, so bruised and battered she could hardly move. She knew she must have broken ribs and she felt the cracked dried blood on her face. There was still a small trickle running down her chin from her lower lip which protruded grotesquely.

Alarmed for the children, she struggled to rise but lay back down as she felt the excruciating pain in her side. "Where is your Daddy? Sunny, you have to get the children and go to your Uncle Thomas's," whispered Lucy.

"It's alright Mama. He's passed out on the ground out back of the house. Guess he was going to the out-house when he fell. We could see him from the woods and watched to be sure he wasn't going to get up. We passed by him and he was snoring," said Jesse.

"Mama we have to get you up and away from here before he wakes up. We can all go to Uncle Thomas's until we can decide what to do," said Sunny.

Lucy knew she could not go to her Uncle's and burden him with their problems but she wanted the children to be safe. "Go in the house and fetch me a piece of paper and pencil. I could never make it to Thomas's in my condition Sunny, you know that. I'll ask Thomas if you kids can stay there for a few days until I know it is safe for you to come home."

"But Mama," protested Sunny. "What about you? Who will take care of you and what if Daddy starts beating you again?"

"I have been through this so many times with your Daddy, although this is probably the worst. He's through with me for awhile but I'm afraid he will remember you kid's jumping on him last night and I don't know what he might do. It's best we handle it this way. I hate for you to have to walk to Thomas' in the dark but you can take the lantern. As long as you stay in the road, with the full moon, you should be fine," said Lucy.

Lucy scribbled her note of explanation and apology to her Uncle and sent the children on their way. She knew the children were exhausted emotionally and physically. She asked Thomas to keep them there for a couple of days until she was better and able to take care of them. She knew her Uncle would not interfere in hers and Junior's affairs. He had long ago given up on doing anything to help Lucy. It wasn't that he didn't care. He just couldn't bear to see the life she had to live and stayed away until she asked for his help.

Once the children were gone, Lucy slowly rose to her feet and made her way into the house, holding her side, a searing pain ripping into her with each step. She reached the wash basin they used to wash their hands and face before eating and looked into the small mirror which hung above the basin. She was not shocked at the face staring back at her. She had long ago grown used to that battered look.

After cleaning her face as best she could, Lucy made her way to the room where the children slept. She crawled into the small bed her two little girls shared. Lucy knew the next few days were going to be extremely hard. She eventually fell asleep with tears of exhaustion running down her face.

Lucy awoke to the sound of Junior stumbling around in the next room. The sun was up already and was shinning through the window above the bed where she lay. Lucy had long ago given up on the idea of "fancy" things like curtains for the windows. It was hard enough just providing the absolute basic necessities.

Lucy wondered why she wasn't afraid of Junior this morning. She lay there pondering this for a moment then realized she just didn't care anymore. Lucy had finally reached her breaking point. She felt dead inside, all hope gone. The only thing that kept her breathing was her children. It was as though there were two Lucy's. The Lucy lying here now, who didn't care if she ever saw another day. Then there was the other Lucy, who loved her children with every fiber of her being. It was the later Lucy who rose from that bed and slowly made her way to face the cause of all her misery.

Junior had changed his clothes and cleaned his face. He looked at Lucy as she slowly entered the room, holding her side. Lucy had learned long ago that Junior wasn't capable of having any feelings of remorse for his actions and expected nothing now. She was a bit surprised as she saw him hang his head a moment as if in shame. That moment was short lived however, as he mumbled "Ain't we gonna have any breakfast this morning?"

Lucy knew he did not know that the children were gone and chose not to mention it. She went about starting the fire in the stove and getting breakfast ready, all the time holding her side. She would gasp with pain each time she turned too quickly and felt the pain rip into her.

"What's wrong with you this morning?" Junior asked, as he sat down in his usual seat at the table.

Lucy would have laughed at that had it not been so painful. "I wouldn't think you would need to ask that question. It should be obvious," said Lucy, somewhat surprised she dared be so bold.

Junior looked at her and Lucy could see the anger in his eyes. He sat staring for a moment and then looked away. The moment had passed and Lucy knew if he was going to have at her again it would have been then.

Lucy sat Junior's breakfast before him and turned to leave the room. She had to put some binding around her chest to help alleviate the pain.

"Ain't you gonna feed the kids this morning? They aught to be out of bed by now. I know it's Saturday but there's still work needs doing," said Junior, stuffing half a biscuit into his mouth.

"I sent them to Thomas' last night. I wanted them to be safe from you. You are lucky you didn't kill Sunny when you kicked him in the head with that boot of yours. And Jesse, he has two black eyes. That should really make you feel proud," said Lucy, bracing for the blow she knew would come.

Junior slowly rose from his chair and stood staring at Lucy for a moment. She stood waiting for the blow but for some reason it didn't come this morning. Junior kicked over his chair and slammed out of the house. Maybe somewhere way deep down inside, Junior did have a soul, Lucy thought.

Three days passed and Lucy slowly improved. She was still sore from the beating and the pain was still there from the ribs, although not quite as severe. Junior had just left for the field when Lucy heard the sound of a vehicle outside. She opened the door to see Thomas and the children coming towards her, looking somewhat apprehensive. The two little girls ran to their mother and hugged her legs. Lucy patted their heads as it was too painful to bend and hug them as she wanted to do.

"Are you all right Lucy?" asked Thomas, coming up the porch steps. "I waited until we thought it was safe to bring the children back. Lucy, I am begging you to leave this place, for yours as well as the children's safety," said Thomas, pleadingly.

"And go where Uncle Thomas? I don't have any way to support myself or the children. You don't have room for all of us at your house. I made the mistake long ago Uncle Thomas, against your wishes, and now I have to pay for it. I am just sorry my children have to pay for that mistake as well. Junior will be all right for awhile. I will just have to be more careful and try to keep the children away from him as much as possible," said Lucy, knowing that was little comfort to Thomas.

Lucy thanked Thomas who left reluctantly telling her they would manage somehow if she changed her mind.

"Are you OK Mama? Where is Daddy?" asked Sunny, looking around for his father.

"He has gone to the fields already. Come on inside and I will fix you something to eat. I want you kids to stay out of your Daddy's way when he comes home, especially until we see how he is going to act towards you after the other night."

Lucy hated the way the kids looked at her as she went about fixing their meal. She knew they loved her but she also knew at times they blamed her for their predicament. That look hurt her more than any of Junior's beatings.

When Junior came home that night, he didn't say a word to Lucy or the children. He went abut his normal routine as though nothing had happened at all. Occasionally Lucy would catch him glancing at Jesse who still showed the signs of the beating Junior had given him. Junior too, still had the marks of the beating his cousin, Maynard had given to him.

After they had all eaten the boys headed off to bed. Junior stuck his head in the bedroom door and said, "You boys better get a good night's sleep. We gotta get up and get to the fields early tomorrow." And with that, things were back to normal. Never an apology or mention of the terrible things he had done to his children or Lucy.

A few weeks later Lucy was spreading rat poison in the corn crib. It seemed the rats were getting more of the corn than the farm animals. She finished with the chore and started back to the house, the box of poison still in her hand. She stepped upon the back step and halted, staring at the box in her hand. Poison, she had poison, right there in her hands, she thought. It could all be ended with just a little of what was in that box. She shook her head, as if to clear such thoughts away. She put the box away and went about her chores, but her mind kept coming back to that box.

When Junior brought the children home that evening, she noticed the boys were exhausted and filthy. Their clothes clung to their bodies from the sweat. Junior still looked fresh as a daisy. When Junior went to the outhouse, Lucy asked Sunny, "Did your father work with you in the fields today?"

"No Maam, He dropped us off there and we didn't see him again until this afternoon at quitting time," responded Junior.

Lucy was furious. How dare he do this to his own children. That night, Lucy lay awake for the longest time. She felt she had no choice. To protect her children, she would do what she had to do. It was the only way out. The decision was made. The next day she would commit murder.

It was Saturday and usually everyone would work only half a day. Sunny and his brothers usually spent the rest of the afternoon with their cousins, swimming in the pond behind their Grandfather's barn or fishing. They asked to spend the night and return home before noon the next day. Lucy knew this would be the opportune time to carry out her plan. She purposefully cooked cabbage because she knew the girls would not touch it. It was one of Junior's favorite vegetables, however. She wasn't sure exactly how much of the rat poison to use. She giggled, almost hysterical, there were no instructions on how to poison one's abusive husband. She decided to cook the cabbage in a beef stock to disguise any flavor the poison might have. The cabbage was ready and Lucy sat down to wait for Junior. She had the girls go to bed a little earlier than usual. They didn't argue as they were good children and usually did as Lucy asked.

Junior came home and flopped down in the chair reserved for him at the head of the table. He did not even bother to wash his hands, Lucy thought. He would die with a dirty face and dirty hands. This almost brought on another fit of giggles and she fought to get control.

"Ain't you gonna eat?" asked Junior, as he shoveled a fork full of cabbage into his mouth. He loved to crumble his cornbread into the cabbage juice and eat that as well so Lucy knew he would get a good dose of the poison.

"We already ate," said Lucy, and busied her self cleaning the dishes the girls had left. She had to keep busy or she would surely go insane, she thought.

Junior finished his meal and went outside to the front porch, as was his habit. Lucy did not know how long it would take for the poison to take effect, so she waited. After a short time, Junior came into the house and announced he was going to bed. Lucy knew this was out of the ordinary and looked at Junior closely. He looked a little pale and was holding his stomach.

Junior undressed and lay down on the bed. Lucy sat up for awhile, not quite sure what to do. The waiting was excruciating. She began to consider the consequences of what she had done. What if someone found out? She would be put away and there would be no one to take care of her children. God, what have I done? She thought.

Little more than an hour had passed when Junior got up from the bed and rushed outside. He was doubled over with pain. Lucy saw him practically running to the outhouse. She waited to see what would happen next. He returned to the house, gulped a large glass of water and fell back into bed. This went on for several hours. Lucy pretended to be reading. She could not bring herself to lie down next to Junior on the bed. Around midnight, Junior was quiet. Lucy tiptoed over to the bed, sure she would find him dead. As she stood looking down at him, however, she saw the slow rise and fall of his chest. The poison had not worked.

Lucy did not know what she felt. She guessed she should be relieved that Junior had not died. At least she did not have to worry about being taken away from her children. Something died in Lucy that night. There was no way out for her and the children. She had no way of supporting her family. She could not drive a car and had no way of getting about if she could find a job. Junior had forced her to sell her Grandmother's house years before. They had moved back into the original house built for them when they were first married. The house had been abandoned by Junior's sister and was now no more than a shack.

The little money her Grandmother had left her was long gone. Their lot was cast. She would just pray and do the best she could for her children until they were adults and could leave this place and their abusive father.

CHAPTER 18

It was a cold blustery day and winter was fast approaching. Lucy knew they had to have fire wood to see them through the cold days ahead. They would need wood for the fireplace as well as the cook stove. Junior and his brothers would saw the logs and haul them to their respective homes. From that point it was Lucy, Sunny and Jesse's job to split the logs into the size needed for the stove and fire place. The girls racked the wood in a stack behind the house. Lucy wondered sometimes why Junior felt no need to help with that part of the job. Sometimes Lucy would be huge with another baby on the way. Still, it was expected of her to help with the wood.

On this day, Lucy and Sunny made their way into the forest behind their house, looking for the stumps of old pine trees. This made a wonderful kindling to use in starting their fires. They had collected as much as they could carry when Sunny asked if they could rest a moment before starting back. Truth was, he liked this quiet time with his mother away from all the other children. They talked about things going on in his life and what he would do after graduating high school.

Lucy moved over to a nearby log which would make a comfortable seat. She raised the axe she was carrying and brought it down with a whack to the log. Her intention was to be sure she did not forget the axe when they were ready to leave. Just as the axe came down, Sunny moved his hand to rest on the log. Too late, Lucy saw Sunny's hand but could not stop the fall of the axe. Blood began to pour from Sunny's hand. Terrified, Lucy grabbed the hand and tried to stop the bleeding. It looked as though three fingers were almost severed. Sunny just stood as if in shock. He didn't appear to be in a lot of pain but Lucy knew the pain would come. She had to stop the bleeding and get him to a doctor fast.

Neither Lucy, nor any of her children had ever been to a doctor. The children had gotten all their immunization shots in school by the county nurse.

Lucy removed her sweater and wrapped Sunny's hand as best she could. She used the sleeve of the sweater as a tourniquet to try and stop the bleeding. By the time they made their way back home, Sunny was feeling weak and was in considerable pain.

Lucy started screaming for help as they drew within shouting distance of the house. Junior, followed by all the other children, came out onto the porch to see what the racket was about.

"We have to get Sunny to the doctor now," cried Lucy, near tears.

"What's the matter with him?" asked Junior, showing little concern.

"I accidentally cut his hand with the axe. It's bad and he has to see a doctor. It's not something your mother can fix this time Junior," cried Lucy. Miss Allie could deliver babies and had even been known to set a bone or two but Lucy knew this was serious.

"Well let's see what it looks like. We don't have any money for a doctor," grumbled Junior as he began to remove Lucy's sweater from Sunny's hand. Even Junior gasped when he got a look at the mess that had been Sunny's hand. Lucy could see now the fingers were cut badly but could possibly be saved if they could get Sunny to the doctor in time.

They had no transportation at the moment and the nearest person who could help them lived a couple of miles away. Lucy instructed Jesse to get one of the mules used for the plowing. She would take Sunny herself if she had to. For once Junior took charge and said he would take Sunny to Charlie Bensons and ask him to take them to the doctor. Lucy did not know if Junior agreed to take Sunny out of concern or if it was because he would have been ashamed for the Bensons to see Lucy ride up on a mule with Sunny instead of him. Lucy suspected it was the latter. She wanted to go with Sunny but knew the Bensons were kind people and would get him where he needed to go.

The hour's drug by as Lucy waited for Junior and Sunny to return. The sun was just dropping behind the horizon of the tree line when Junior returned. Lucy was startled when she saw Sunny wasn't with him.

"What happened? Where's Sunny?" asked Lucy, almost afraid of the answer.

"He's at the New Albany Hospital," replied Junior. "Charlie said it wouldn't do any good to take him to the doctor's office. Said we needed to take him to the emergency room where he could get looked after right away. They fixed up his hand but wanted to keep him over night to keep an eye on him," said Junior. "I have to get the mule put away then I'll need something to eat. I ain't had anything all day and I'm starved," said Junior as he started for the door.

"But is he going to be all right," asked Lucy, needing reassurance.

"I said he was didn't I?" snapped Junior.

"But when will he be coming home?" asked Lucy.

"Charlie told me he would run me over tomorrow around noon to pick him up. They asked all kinds of questions at that hospital. I told them I didn't have any money but they had to take care of Sunny anyway. None of this would have happened if you had been watching what you were doing," grumbled Junior, as he turned and left the house.

Lucy sank into a nearby chair and sobbed, she didn't know if it was from relief that Sunny was going to be all right or the guilt she felt. Junior didn't need to remind her it was her fault. She had been blaming herself all day. She never stopped to think, if Junior had been doing the job himself as he should have been, she would not have been out there in the woods in the first place.

Sunny came home the next day with his hand in a cast and a peculiar looking thing attached to his middle finger. Apparently it was damaged the worst and needed extra support until the bone and tissue could heal. When the cast was removed several weeks later the doctor assured Sunny he would eventually regain the full use of his hand.

CHAPTER 19

The proudest day of Lucy's life was the day Sunny graduated high school. It had been a long hard road but they had made it. Sunny had already signed up for the army and left the day after graduation. He had forty dollars of his pay sent home to his mother each month. This was a Godsend for Lucy. It helped her pay the electric bill and buy school supplies and necessities for the other children.

Jesse graduated next. A manufacturing plant had opened in the little town nearby. Junior had plan's of putting Jesse to work there. The money would come in nicely he thought. He and Jesse came to blows the morning Jesse explained he would be leaving. He had been accepted into the Air Force and was leaving the next week. Junior was furious. He could see his work force dwindling away. He yelled at Jesse, "You're not going anywhere except to that factory to work." Jesse dared to talk back to his father and received a blow across the mouth from Junior's fist. Something snapped in Jesse and he tore into his father as if he would kill him. Jesse had always taken what Junior dished out and now all that rage boiled to the surface.

The fight only lasted a couple of minutes but Junior was left lying on the floor, blood flowing from his nose.

"Get the hell out of here and never come back," Junior screamed.

Jesse just looked at his father with contempt and walked out the door. He went to stay with his Great Uncle Thomas until the following week, when he left for the Air Force.

Lucy had been watching the fight, to afraid to move. She was afraid Junior would kill her son. When the fight was over, she let out her breath and followed Jesse outside. She told him she was sorry for everything. "I am proud of you and your brother and I love you more than anything. You are your own man now and you will never have to be around your father again if you choose not to." Jesse left and Lucy did not see him again for four years.

CHAPTER 20

The years slipped by and more children were born as the older children finished school and left. None of them stayed more than a few days after graduating. Lucy had insisted they finish high school no matter what. Her first daughter, Jenny, left the night she graduated and never came back. Lucy had suspected Junior of trying to molest Jenny but could never catch him at it. As Jenny grew into her teens she would catch Junior looking at her in peculiar ways. She noticed how Jenny always tried to avoid being alone with her father. She hated to see her children leave and she missed them dreadfully but was relieved they would never be hurt by Junior again.

Lucy guessed she would miss Jenny the most as she had been a tremendous help to her in the care of the younger children. It seemed there was always a baby in the house. Jenny was a quiet shy girl who loved to draw pictures on every scrap of paper she could find. Lucy had no idea Jenny dreamed of being a famous artist some day.

As Jenny grew older Lucy became more dependent on her and gave her more responsibilities. One such task that fell to Jenny was the Christmas shopping for the younger children each year. No matter how hard the times, Lucy always managed to put aside a little money to be used for that purpose. They picked black berries in the summer and sold them. Lucy managed to sneak a few dollars from the money they made working for the various farmers in the area. Sometimes Junior would be late picking them up and Lucy would be given the money for their labors. She would tuck a few dollars away before Junior arrived.

Jenny would always manage to get at least one small item for each child even if it was only a coloring book and crayons. The boys all got firecrackers which they loved. There would always be a bag of orange slice candy, nuts, apples and oranges. This was the only time the children ever had candy or fruit. Jenny told her mother years later that she never smelled oranges and apples that she didn't think of Christmas. Another thing they always got at Christmas was a new toothbrush and a tube of toothpaste. These were luxury items and the children were glad to get them.

Junior no longer owned the twenty five acres his father had given him when he had married Lucy. He had sold the house and land and moved them into an old run down tenant house on Mr. Roy West's place. Lucy and the remaining children worked in the fields for Mr. West and in return he allowed them to live in the house for nothing. During harvest season, Junior would take Lucy and the children to the field then go on his merry way.

Sometimes Lucy would still have a nursing baby and would have to take the baby to the fields with her. She would place the baby on a pallet at the end of the cotton rows and check on it each time she finished a row. It was a horrible way to live but as always in Lucy's life, she had done what had to be done.

As the farmers in the area became more modernized and started using automated cotton pickers, there was little demand for Junior and his brood of children. Mr. West came by one day and told Lucy they would have to be moving. The county was building a new road and the route was running right through the field where the house sat. They were given a few days to find another place to live. Lucy was totally worn out. All the child bearing and abuse from Junior had taken a toll. Once again, she was being asked to uproot her children and move on.

Junior came home and announced he had found a house near the meat packing plant where Lucy could probably get a job. The plant was about a mile away from the house and she could walk if need be. Lucy wondered why she would be the one to go work there and not Junior. She had learned a long time ago to keep such thoughts to herself.

The move was made and Lucy applied for a job at the plant. It was a small business which supplied sausage, pork chops and other cuts of pork to the local grocery stores.

To Lucy's surprise she was given the job. Her duties would be to work in the area where pork was ground, seasoned and made into sausage.

The first day Lucy went to work, she knew her life had changed. She could have some independence now and she was determined Junior would not take all her money. Junior could barely write his name so Lucy knew he would not be able to read her paychecks, therefore, he would not know how much money she made. She went into the owner's office that first morning, so nervous she felt faint, and asked him to please keep the amount of her pay between them. Mr. Cantor suspected why Lucy asked him this and assured her it was no one else's business and would be kept between the two of them.

Her first day at work went by so fast she hardly knew where the time went. The area where Lucy worked was shared by only one other person, a black woman named Coretta.

This was the beginning of the sixties and the Civil Rights movement was just getting under way. Lucy was a little shy around Coretta at first but soon found herself laughing and talking abut things she had never shared with anyone. She enjoyed every minute and hardly noticed the pain in her back as she lifted the heavy tubs of ground pork. She did not care that Coretta was black, for the first time in her life, she had a friend.

The days flew by. It was exhausting for Lucy, working at the meat plant all day and taking care of the household chores at night. Junior never lifted a finger to help around the house. Lucy still did not have water in the house and laundry was an all day job reserved for Saturdays. After the laundry was done, she would save the big tub of rinse water for the children's weekly bath. During the week the children washed their faces, hands and feet before going to bed. That was the extent of their personal hygiene. Lucy dreamed of living in a house with running water some day, but knew there was very little chance of that happening. Still, it would be glorious to have one of those electric washing machines, she thought

Junior came home one day with a radio and all the children gathered round as he plugged it into the one light socket by the front door. Lucy did not ask where or how he came about having the radio but found her self as excited as the children. It became their favorite pastime. They would gather round and listen to the Grand Ole Opry every Saturday night. That radio opened up a whole new world for Lucy. She began to pay attention to the news reports and was astonished at some of the things she heard. There were reports of violence toward blacks as the Civil Rights movement really took hold. Lucy and Coretta steered away from this subject, not wanting to jeopardize their friendship. There was an unspoken understanding between Coretta & Lucy. It would be unacceptable for them to visit in each others homes. Coretta had two sons of her own who attended the all black school. There was talk of sending the black children to the white schools and Coretta felt a sense of dread. She wanted her children to have a good education but feared what might happen to them if they were forced into the white schools.

One day Coretta came to work and mumbled a "morning" to Lucy and went about preparing for the day's work. Lucy knew something was wrong as Coretta was usually in a good mood and sang out a "Good Morning" as she breezed through the door. After an hour of silence, Lucy walked over and placed an arm around Coretta's shoulders. Before Lucy could say anything, Coretta burst into tears, throwing herself into Lucy's arms.

"Oh Coretta, what ever is the matter," asked Lucy, real concern in her voice.

"I'm sorry Lucy. I didn't mean to act this way but I am so mad and upset. I feel so angry sometimes but I feel helpless to do anything about it," said Coretta, wiping her tears on her apron.

"What happened Coretta?" asked Lucy, as she sat down beside her friend. They didn't worry about Mr. Cantor catching them sitting down on the job. He seldom came into their area as the women were hard workers and always got their work done.

"My nephew, Clarence, was walking home from work last night. He's usually home before dark but Mr. Jenkins kept him later than usual. They were trying to get all the hay in the barn before the expected

rain tomorrow. Clarence was walking down the highway when these men drove by and started yelling and
cursing at him. One of them threw a beer bottle at
Clarence and barely missed his head. Clarence said
he thought they were gone but they turned around
in the middle of the road and came back." Coretta
paused, trying to get control of her emotions.

"What they did to that boy shouldn't happen to anyone. He was just a young boy trying to help his folks
out, Lucy. They made him pull his clothes off and run
around the field there by the road for awhile. Clarence
said he tried to run away but they chased him down.
After beating him, they tied his hands behind his back
and strung him up to a tree limb. He stood on his
tiptoes for hours then couldn't hold out any longer.
One of Sheriff Martin's deputies, out on night patrol,
found him strung up to that tree," Coretta finished, a
new rush of tears streaming down her face.

"How is he now Coretta?" Lucy gently asked.

"Oh, he is still in the hospital over in Holly Springs.
He had to have numerous stitches and both shoulders were dislocated. I tell you Lucy, when Earl heard
what happened to his nephew, I thought he would go
crazy he was so mad. He went over to the hospital to
see Clarence to find out who had done this to him.
Clarence wouldn't tell, whether from fear for himself
or his family, I don't know. Anyway, I'm ashamed to
say I was glad he didn't tell because I know Earl would
not let it go. No offense meant to you Lucy, but you

know a black man is always in the wrong no matter what and Earl would surely have gotten into trouble."

"I'm so sorry Coretta. I don't know how one person can be so cruel to another regardless of color. Maybe times are changing for the better Coretta. I heard that Reverend King talking on the radio the other day and I have to say I got chills listening to him. Junior came in and made me turn the radio off so I didn't get to hear all his speech but I think he is the hope of your people Coretta. Maybe in years to come things like this won't happen anymore. At least if they do, they won't go unpunished," Lucy finished.

"Thank you Lucy. I am sorry to burden you with all this. I know you got problems of your own. Seems everybody got their own worries in some way or another," Coretta sighed, rising from her seat.

Lucy patted her friends hand in reassurance and said, "Guess we had better get back to work."

The incident seemed to close the gap in the friendship between the two women. Coretta had a better understanding of Lucy's true feelings and felt comfortable discussing any subject with her now.

Coretta's husband worked at the sawmill along with several other black men. It was hard work and paid very little but not much was offered for black men in the south. Most of them did cheap manual labor such as the sawmill or share cropped for the local farmers. Earl was good to his wife and children but sometimes became angry and depressed that he could not provide better for them. At these times, he would go by Sara Mae Johnson's house and pick up a pint of liquor.

Sara Mae sold the liquor for the Smith brother's over in Union County who brought her a new supply weekly. The Union County Sheriff knew about the Smith Brother's steel but looked the other way as they gave him a cut of their profits. Sara Mae was also known to "entertain" any of the good ole boys who dropped by with a need for company. Junior was a regular customer, not for the liquor, but for Sara Mae's company.

Late one afternoon Junior decided to go visit Sara Mae for awhile. He checked his pocket and found he only had one dollar. His income dwindled down considerably after all the crops were harvested and the kid's could no longer work. Still, Sara Mae liked his love making he thought. She would probably be glad to take the dollar he had instead of the five she normally charged.

He pulled up in front of the house and found Sara Mae sitting on the front porch, her dress hiked up around her thighs. She's hot and ready he thought as he got out of the old truck and approached her. Truth was she was hot all right but not for Junior or any other man, still a girl had to do what a girl had to do.

"What you up to Junior?" asked Sara Mae, as Junior flopped down on the porch beside her, wiping the sweat from his brow.

"Oh just thought I'd come by and see how my favorite gal is doing," said Junior, as he ran his hand up Sara Mae's thigh.

Taking the hint, Sara Mae got up and led Junior inside, closing the door behind her. She held out her hand for the money. She always collected up front. She did not offer her services for nothing. Junior pulled her to him and started pulling at her underwear.

"Take it easy Junior. We have plenty of time. Just hand over the money and we can get down to business." Junior reluctantly pulled out the dollar and placed it in Sara Mae's hand. She looked at the money and began to laugh. "Come on Junior, you know I charge five dollars. No money, no honey," Sara Mae said, and backed away from Junior. This infuriated him. How dare her get him all riled up and then laugh at him. He would treat her like the whore she was and with that, grabbed her by the hair and dragged her towards the bed.

Sara Mae was no puritan for sure but she would not be forced to do something if she did not want to. Having worked on a farm during her child hood Sara Mae was quite strong and she fought Junior with all her strength. She was like a mad woman, clawing and kicking but Junior was not deterred. The more Sara Mae fought, the more aroused and angry he became. Sara Mae hit Junior in the nose with her fist and the blood flew. This enraged Junior and he began to beat her with his fist. He could not stop himself. Blow after blow landed on the helpless woman's face. Junior seemed unaware she was now unconscious. He entered her and finished the sexual act in seconds as he choked the last breath of life from her.

He lay on top of her for a few seconds, panting as if he had run for miles. He raised himself up and looked down at the now dead woman. "Sara Mae, quit your fooling around now," Junior said, as he stood up to leave. "You asked for it you know. All you had to do was take the dollar. I thought you liked me Sara Mae," Junior said, as he pulled his pants up.

Junior looked closer at the woman now, the first stirrings of fear growing in his stomach. He touched the side of Sara Mae's neck and found no pulse. She's dead, he thought. I have to get out of here before somebody sees me. He looked at his shirt and saw it was spattered with blood. He touched his face and felt the blood still seeping from his nose. He knew most of the blood had come from Sara Mae. There were several scratches on his arms and his ear had a big bruise where she had bitten him. He had to get home before someone saw him he thought, as he rushed out of the house, leaving the door open behind him.

The children were all in bed by the time Junior arrived home. Lucy was just putting away the last of the supper dishes when Junior bounded through the door. Lucy took one look at him and gasped. "What in the world happened to you?" she asked. She could see Junior was not himself and was unsure how she should react. She had learned over the years it did not take much provocation for Junior to feel justified in punching her in the face.

"None of your business woman," snarled Junior. "If anybody comes around here asking questions, you tell them I was here with you all evening," said Junior, as he began to strip off the bloody clothes. Not even bothering to dress, he went outside and built a fire under Lucy's wash pot. He threw the clothes in the fire and stood watching as the last threads were burned. Lucy stood by and watched, a feeling of dread coming over her.

"What have you done Junior? Why will anyone be asking questions about where you were this evening? I won't lie for you Junior. What ever you have done, it has nothing to do with me or the kids and I will keep it that way," said Lucy, with more courage than she felt.

Junior glared at Lucy with a look she knew all too well. He stood inches from her face and hissed, "If you care anything at all about them brats inside, you'll do as I say. Kids fall out of trees you know, and break their necks. They are always having accidents. Just remember that if anybody comes poking around here. I was here all evening, got it."

Lucy nodded, cold with fear, not for herself, but for her children. She knew he was capable of anything at this point.

If he played his cards right, he could get away with this, Junior thought, as he stomped inside and fell into bed.

CHAPTER 21

The sawmill where Earl worked was near Sara Mae's house. Earl had to walk by on his way home. It was Friday and he had just gotten paid. Exhausted, he decided to stop by Sara Mae's and pick up his usual pint of liquor. Earl had never entered the house before. Sara Mae would fetch the liquor while he stood waiting on the porch steps. Today, however, Earl did not see any sign of Sara Mae. He called out but got no response. Noticing the door ajar, Earl stepped up on the porch calling out, "Miss Sara Mae, you in there?" Getting no response Earl, approached the door and looked inside, still calling out. He gasped as he saw Sara Mae lying on the bed. She had a small bed placed in the living room for her "men visitors." She would not have them soiling the sheets in the bedroom where she slept.

Earl could see the fly's buzzing about Sara Mae's bloodied head and knew she was dead. Terrified, he backed out the door, stumbling and falling as he stepped off the porch. He hit the ground with a thud, the side of his face hitting a sharp rock on the ground. Blood started gushing from the wound. Still dazed from the blow, Earl rose from the ground just as a car came round the curve in view of the house. "My God," he thought, I have to get out of here. They will think I killed this woman." Terrified, he ran from the house into the vast expanse of woods that spread behind Sara Mae's house, but not before the driver of the car saw him.

Twin brothers, Ronny and Randy Simpson had dropped out of school at the age of sixteen. Two years later, they were no stranger to the county jail. They too, liked to partake of Sara Mae's company as well as her whiskey. It was the weekend and they had a few dollars to spend. They had worked all week helping Mr. Conley load hay bales onto the back of a trailer. The boys then hoisted the hay up into the loft of Mr. Conley's barn. The hay was used during the winter to feed the farm animals. It was hot, dusty work but it was about all the boys could find. They were expecting to be drafted into the army at any time, so decided to live it up until then.

Just as their vehicle came in view of Sara Mae's house, they saw Earl take the tumble off the steps of her porch. They thought that quite funny until Earl got up and raced into the woods as if the devil himself was chasing him.

"What's that nigger up to?" asked Ronny, as he brought the old jalopy to a halt. The boys got out of the car and Randy yelled out, "Hey Earl, what's your hurry?" Earl made no reply and raced out of sight into the woods.

The boys went up the steps calling out for Sara Mae. Hearing nothing, they walked up to the open door and stopped abruptly as they saw Sara Mae's body lying lifeless on the bed.

"Oh my God, that nigger's done killed Sara Mae," whispered Randy. "We got to go get the Sheriff," said Ronny as he pulled his brother down the steps toward the car.

"They might think we done it," said Randy.

"No they won't if we tell them what we saw. That Earl was running so fast he's probably in the next county by now. He wouldn't have run if he hadn't been the one that done it," reasoned Ronny.

The boys wasted no time in getting to the Sheriff's office. They were both trying to talk at them same time and Sheriff Martin, growing aggravated, finally shouted for them both to hush. "Now, one at a time, tell me what's got you so riled up, you first Randy."

"It was that nigger, Earl Bates, that works at the sawmill, he's done killed Sara Mae," said Randy, feeling important that he was allowed to speak first.

"What's he talking about Ronny? Tell me the whole story from start to finish," said Sheriff Martin. There had not been a murder in this county in thirty eight years. About all he had to worry about was the occasional drunk beating up his wife on a Saturday night. This would be big news if what the boys said was true.

"Well we went by Sara Mae's house and saw that Earl come running out the door like a scalded dog. He fell off the porch and then got up and ran into the woods when he saw us. Seeing Sara Mae's door open, we decided to stop and check on her," said Ronny, leaving out the part about their plans to purchase whiskey.

"We called out to Sara Mae and when she didn't answer we looked in the door cause it was standing wide open. We saw Sara Mae lying on the bed with blood all over her head. We just know she was dead cause the fly's was startin to buzz around her," Ronny finished.

"Guess we had better get out there and take a look. You say Earl ran into the woods behind Sara Mae's? I'll call Oliver and Grady to meet us there." Oliver and Grady were his Deputy's and it sounded as if he might be needing them. "You boy's don't mind following me back over there do you?" asked the Sheriff. He wanted to keep the boys near by until he knew exactly what was going on.

By the time Sheriff Martin arrived at Sara Mae's house, half dozen men were tramping in and out of the place. Many of the locals still had party lines and news spread fast, especially news of this type.

"What the hell you men doing here?" asked Sheriff Martin, knowing his crime scene, if there was one, was completely destroyed.

"We heard that nigger Earl Bates done killed Sara Mae. We come to help hunt him down," said Johnny

Lunsford, a big raw boned man who looked like he might enjoy "hunting a man down" as he put it.

"This is the business of the Sheriff's Department and you men should not even be here. Just look what a mess you've made of things," said Sheriff Martin, pushing past the men congregated on Sara Mae's porch.

Sara Mae was indeed dead it was determined. Sheriff Martin notified the proper officials and with the help of the two deputies, went about noting anything they thought might be useful as evidence. It looked like there was no question about who had done the deed in the mind's of the men still loitering about outside the house. Comments like "we need to go get that nigger and string him up" and "the only good nigger is a dead nigger." Sheriff Martin knew the situation could easily get out of hand if he did not nip it in the bud and quickly.

"I am telling you men to go on home now. Me and my Deputies will take care of this business. I appreciate your concern but I need you to leave." The men moved out of the yard but still stood around grumbling as the body was taken away.

One of Junior's brothers had ridden over to tell him the news about Sara Mae. He sat on the porch telling Junior about the terrible thing that had befallen her. "They say that nigger, Earl Bates, is the one that did it," he informed Junior. Lucy had been standing just inside the door and heard the news about Sara Mae. She was shaking and upon hearing Earl's name mentioned, her knees gave way and she sank to the floor. She knew Junior had something to do with this and now her dear friend, Coretta's husband, would be blamed for it. Was there no end to the evil this man she had married could do, she thought.

"The Simpson boy's say Earl ran into the woods behind Sara Mae's house. If the Sheriff don't find him at home, we know where to go looking for him," said Junior's brother.

"I say we get everybody together tonight and go out there and find him," said Junior.

It had been rumored there was a secret group of men who called themselves "The Militia." These men went out late at night and burned crosses in the yards of any black, or white for that matter, who supported the Civil Rights movement. Lucy had seen the brown uniform Junior had brought home one day and tucked away under the bed. She now suspected Junior was a part of this group. She had read the story in the local paper of how a house had been burned, the people inside barley escaping with their lives. It was suspected the fire was no accident. It was being used by a group of whites who had ridden buses down from the north to march the streets in support of the Civil Rights movement.

"We'll leave right now and start getting everybody together," said Junior's brother. "If the Sheriff don't get him first we'll find him." Noticing the bruise on Junior's ear, Grady asked, "what happened to your ear there bub?"

"Oh I bumped it on the door sill in the dark last night," answered Junior, tugging on the sleeves of his shirt. He hoped no one would find it odd that he would be wearing a long sleeved shirt in the warm weather.

Junior came inside and saw Lucy sitting on the floor near the door. He knew she had overheard the conversation and could see the look of contempt and accusation in her eyes. He pulled Lucy to her feet by her hair and whispered in her ear, "Remember what we talked about earlier." He released her but not before slamming the back of her head against the wall.

Lucy felt as if she would go mad. She had to protect her children, but at the same time, she knew what this would do to her friend, Coretta. Earl and Coretta had two sons and Lucy knew they loved their father very much. From what Coretta had told her, Lucy knew Earl was a good husband and father. Maybe she could get word to someone and Junior would be arrested before he could hurt her children, she reasoned. They would be rid of him for good, she thought. But what if they did not arrest him, then what? The answer was too horrible for Lucy to imagine. In the end, she could only hope Sheriff Martin would find Earl first and he would be able to prove his innocence somehow. There would be no sleep for Lucy this night.

Sheriff Martin and one of his Deputies went to Earl's house in hopes he had returned there. Sheriff Martin felt he had no choice but to arrest Earl when he found him. There had been witnesses to his presence at the crime scene, and he did flee as if guilty.

Earl made his way through the woods working his way towards his house. He had to keep away from the road where he might be seen. He was terrified because he knew without question he would be blamed for Sara Mae's death. He was a black man and he had been seen running from the house. Briars and limbs slashed across Earl's face and arms as he ran heedless through the forest. He reached the edge of the woods in back of his house and was about to step into the clearing when he saw Sheriff Martin pull up in front of the house. Earl backed back into the woods and watched. Coretta and Earl's two children stepped out on the porch. He could hear the conversation from where he hid and his blood ran cold. Just as he suspected, they were searching for him.

"Evenin Coretta, Earl home from work yet?" asked Sheriff Martin. He did not want to alert her as to the reason for his visit until he could determine what Coretta knew.

"No Sir, he ain't home yet. Should be here any minute though. Is there anything wrong?" asked Coretta, a feeling of dread descending upon her.

Sheriff Martin had known Coretta most of her life and he felt sure she was telling the truth. "Well we need to talk to him Coretta if he comes home. He was seen earlier this evening running away from Sara Mae's house. The Simpson twins saw him and checked to see if anything was wrong. It seems someone beat poor Sara Mae to death this afternoon."

"Oh Lordy mercy," cried Coretta. "He would never hurt that woman, and you know that Sheriff. My Earl is a good man and he ain't never hurt no one," said Coretta, crying and wringing her hands.

"Never the less, Coretta, we need to talk to him. If he comes home you tell him to wait right here. I'll be back later to check on him. A bunch of the local's were gathered outside Sara Mae's house, blood in their eyes. I want to be sure nothing happens to Earl until we can get at the truth of what happened to Sara Mae," said Sheriff Martin, turning to leave.

Earl heard the entire conversation and knew he had to leave. He knew he would be arrested for Sara Mae's murder. A trial for a black man in the south in the early sixties was a joke. He was usually judged by an all white jury and it would take a miracle to save him. There was nothing left for him to do. He could not leave without letting Coretta know he was innocent. He would not have his children thinking he was a murderer.

Earl slipped out of the woods and rushed in the back door of the house. Coretta screamed and ran to him. "Earl, the Sheriff done been here looking for you. He says that Sara Mae is dead and some people think you did it. What are we going to do Earl? What are we going to do?" she cried, clinging to him.

"I had nothing to do with hurting that woman, Coretta. You know that. I just stopped there to get my pint and I found her dead. Them Simpson boys saw me leaving and they must have told the Sheriff I did it. You know I can't stay here until they find who did this," said Earl, gently pulling Coretta's arms from around his neck. "I couldn't leave without telling you what happened, but I have to go now. Pack me some food and I will grab a few clothes. I'll go to Alabama and stay with my brother until they catch the person who did this."

Coretta knew he was right. Sheriff Martin was a fair man but he could only do so much. If Earl went to trial she knew what would happen. She also knew of the secret group of men who had been causing terror among the black community. She could only imagine what they would do to Earl if they found him before the Sheriff. Still crying, she quickly sacked up the little food she could find and gathered the boys to say good by. The children clung to their father, everyone crying now, as he moved to the door.

"How will you get there Earl?" asked Coretta.

"I will have to stick to the woods until I get out of the county, then I'll call Sampson to come get me. I'll lay low somewhere until he can make the trip." Unlike most black's, Earl's brother had a vehicle. The little town where Sampson lived in Alabama was just across the Mississippi, Alabama line. He could reach Earl by evening the next day if Earl made it out of the county.

"I'll get word to you somehow Coretta that I made it to Sampson's all right. You just tell the Sheriff when he comes back that I never came home," said Earl, as he rushed out the door and into the night.

CHAPTER 22

It was a clear night with a full moon but still, moving about in the thick woods was difficult. Earl had brought with him a flash light but was reluctant to use it for fear it might be seen. Occasionally, he had to resort to the flash light, however, as he lost his bearings and had to backtrack to get back on the trail. There was an old logging road that worked it's way through the woods but had not been used in years. It was grown up now with small trees and undergrowth but a person could follow it easily had it been daylight. The logging road came out on the main highway about eight miles from Earl's house. He would follow the woods parallel to the highway until he could reach the next town. He had been there several times delivering lumber from the saw mill and knew of a pay phone on the edge of town. After calling his brother, he would slip back into the woods and wait for him there. It was a good plan but Earl did not know about the bloodhound belonging to Albert Mason, the leader of the feared "Militia."

Junior and Grady met up with the other Malitia members at their usual meeting place. Word had gotten around and the men had worked themselves up to an angry frenzy by the time Junior and Grady joined the group. "We got to catch us a murderin nigger tonight boys," said Albert, a look of sheer glee in his eyes. He was a cruel man who beat his wife and children regularly, yet these men seemed to look up to him and followed his every word. This said a lot about the men in the group. Truth was, most of them were ignorant cowards who would never confront a man alone.

"I bet he is at his house by now or at least went by there. My old lady works with Earl's wife and she says they are pretty close. He wouldn't leave without seeing her first," said Junior, feeling important that he knew some bit of personal information.

"All right then boys, let's load up and drive out that way. We'll park in the field by old man Carter's barn and walk to the house. We don't want to spook him. There's always the chance the Sheriff might still be there too," said Albert. "We'll take old Roscoe here with us. He can pick up his trail if he has been there."

Whooping and hollering, the men all loaded up and spun out onto the road, spewing gravel and a cloud of dust behind them. They parked their vehicles and made their way to Earl's house. They could see a dim light through the window but no vehicle so they knew the Sheriff was not around. Grady made his way up to the window and peeped inside where he saw only Coretta, sitting with her head in her hands. He could hear moans of anguish coming from inside the house and knew Earl had been there but was probably gone. He backed away from the house and the men stood about whispering, deciding what to do. It was decided time was wasting and they would take the direct approach. They would all gather on the porch before knocking on the door, knowing it would terrify poor Coretta into telling them anything they wanted to know.

Albert pounded on the door as Junior and Grady peered in through the window. They saw the look of fear on Coretta's face as she rose and slowly made her way to the door. Maybe it was Sheriff Martin come back, she thought as she opened the door with dread. She cried out in fear as she saw the group of men standing on her small porch. Word had gotten around the black community about the brown shirted devils terrorizing their friends and families. Coretta never expected to see them standing here on her porch, however.

"What you men want?" asked Coretta, sounding bolder than she felt. Her knees were trembling but she was determined not to let it show. She knew this had something to do with Earl and she had to be strong for her husband and her children.

"We looking for Earl, Coretta," said Albert. "He's done killed Sara Mae this evening and the Sheriff's got us looking for him," Albert lied.

"Earl is not here and I know Sheriff Martin don't have you looking for him cause he done been here and is coming back any minute," said Coretta, hoping this would scare them away.

"Is that so? Well you don't mind if we look around a bit then do you?" said Junior, as he pushed his way into the house, followed by the others.

"You ain't got no right coming into my house like this," shouted Coretta, gathering her crying children to her.

The house was small and it took only a few minutes to determine Earl was not there. "Where is he Coretta? We know he has been here. We just want to help him," lied Grady.

"I'm telling you he ain't been here," cried Coretta.

"We ain't gonna get nothin out of her. Grab that shirt over there, Junior. We'll give old Roscoe a sniff and if he's been here we'll pick up his trail somewhere outside for sure," ordered Albert.

Grabbing the shirt, the men made their way outside the house and watched as Albert coaxed old Roscoe to smell the shirt. The dog sniffed for a few minutes and the men made their way around the house, watching for signs from Roscoe that he may have picked up Earl's scent. They came to the back steps and Roscoe let out a yelp and pulled on his leash, jerking Albert near off his feet.

"He's got it boy's. Everybody grab your guns and follow me. We gonna catch us a coon tonight."

Coretta and her children watched in terror as the men lit out through the woods in the direction Earl had taken not an hour earlier. She could see the beams from their flash lights as they made their way through the woods and could hear the shouts and laughter.

She knew these men would have no mercy for her husband if they were able to catch him.

She sank to her knees, pulling the boys with her. Coretta prayed as she had never prayed before.

Sheriff Martin returned to Coretta's about an hour after the men left. He found Coretta still sitting in the floor with her children asleep next to her, their heads resting in her lap. Tears streamed down her face as she rocked back and forth but not a sound was heard.

"Coretta, what's wrong? Did Earl come back home?" asked Sheriff Martin, kneeling in front of the distraught woman.

Coretta looked at Sheriff Martin with a look he would never forget. It was a look of sheer hopelessness. "Yes he come back Sheriff Martin. He told me he never killed that woman and I believe him. He was afraid to stay here until you find who done it so he left about two hours ago."

"But he didn't need to run Coretta. If he is innocent we will find the person who did it, but in the mean time I have to talk to him," said Sheriff Martin. "Come on Coretta, let me help you up and you need to put those children to bed.

There was something soothing about Sheriff Martin's voice and Coretta slowly reached up to grasp the hand offered to her. She gently lifted her children and placed them on their bed, trying not to wake them. She squared her shoulders and turned to face Sheriff Martin. If there was any hope for her husband it would be through this kind man. She had to tell him where Earl had gone and about the men who followed him.

"Sheriff Martin, you seem like a kind man but you have no idea what it's like to be black in the south, or maybe you do, but just can't do anything about it. I don't know, but Earl felt he had no choice but to run. The problem is, those men came about an hour ago and took out through the woods after him. They had this dog and he is chasing Earl's scent. I am afraid of what they will do if the catch him Sheriff. They had guns and I heard them yellin they was gonna "hang them a nigger," said Coretta, sinking into a nearby chair, exhausted.

Startled at this news, Sheriff Martin knew he had to act quickly. He went to his patrol car and radioed for his deputies to meet him at Earl's house ASAP. It would help in determining how serious the matter was if he knew who all was in the group chasing Earl. He returned to the house, pulled up a chair, and sat down next to Coretta. "Did you know any of those men Coretta?" asked the Sheriff.

"I knew most of their faces and a lot by name," said Coretta, picturing the faces in her mind. "There was the man with the dog, Albert Mason, I believe his name is. There was Junior McGregor and his brother Grady. I can probably remember the other names if I give it some thought. I was just so afraid and the boy's were crying," said Coretta, aggravated that she could not name all the men for the Sheriff.

Seeing how distraught the poor woman was, Sheriff Martin decided to leave her alone for awhile. "I will wait outside for my Deputies, Coretta. Give it some more thought and jot down any other names you can think of. As soon as the Deputies arrive we will be going after the men. Can you show me which direction they went?"

Coretta pointed to an area between two large trees. "There, Earl was going to take that old logging road over to the main highway. He was gonna call his brother in Alabama to come get him once he got to the next town." Coretta felt no need to conceal Earl's route or his plans. She felt it might be the only way to save his life. At least in the Sheriff's custody he might have a chance.

"Please find him for me Sheriff. He only ran because he was afraid. He did not kill that woman."

"I will do my very best Coretta. Try to get some rest and see after your children. I will come and let you know as soon as I know something."

CHAPTER 23

Sheriff Martin was so angry he could bite nails. He sat in his squad car waiting for his Deputies trying to sort it all out. He should have known something like this would happen. Sometimes he was ashamed to be from the south. Would these backwards, ignorant people ever change, he thought. Probably not, he thought, at least not until they were forced to. Generations of the same backward thinking made it difficult to change people. He used to be the same way until a stint in Vietnam had taught him different. There, color made no difference. He became friends with a black boy from Arkansas and that same boy died while trying to save his life. He had vowed to try and make a difference when he returned home. When he became Sheriff, he vowed everyone would be treated fairly, regardless of color and so far he had a reputation of being so.

Shaking his head to clear his thoughts, Sheriff Martin knew he had to come up with a plan to find Earl before that gang of imbeciles chasing him. Earl had an hour's head start on them but might not be moving as quickly. He had no way of knowing he was being chased. He could hear the siren on his Deputies vehicle now and got out of the car.

"What's up Sheriff," asked Jerry Thompson, as he leaped out of the car.

"Earl came home after I left earlier. Coretta says he swears Sara Mae was dead when he got to her house. Says he just stopped by to pick up a pint of whiskey, which very well may be the case. Our problem is, that Albert Mason and his bunch of idiots have gone chasing after Earl through the woods. Coretta says Earl was taking that old logging road over to the main highway. If we hurry we may be able to stop this thing and get to Earl first. Jerry, you and Maynard take the squad car and go over to where that logging road comes out on the highway. Wait there. If Earl comes out, nab him and take him straight to the jail. We have to keep him safe until we get the straight of this thing. I'm going to go after them through the woods. I think I can travel faster alone. If I need you, I'll call you on the radio. You can come in the logging road from the other side. Let's move it," said Sheriff Martin, anxious to get started.

Junior and his buddies ran through the woods, stopping every once in awhile for Roscoe to regain the scent. At times it seemed like Earl was going in circles. Maybe he was getting confused in the dark, they reasoned. Junior's mind was racing as he ran. He had to be sure Earl never made it out of these woods alive. If he was dead, it would just be assumed he was the one who killed Sara Mae and Junior would be in the clear.

After all, people would think, if he wasn't guilty why did he run away.

Earl rushed through the woods, keeping his flashlight on all the time now. He felt sure it could not be seen, the deeper he went into the woods. Of course he was unaware of the danger approaching behind him. Occasionally he would stop and rest on a stump from a long ago hewn tree. It was on such a stump he was sitting when he first heard the sounds of a barking dog. Maybe it was coon hunters, he thought. This area of woods was used by some of the locals for that purpose. Earl never saw the sport in chasing a poor animal up a tree, only to watch the dogs rip it apart as it hit the ground.

The sounds were getting closer now and Earl felt sure he heard voices. Sheer terror coursed through him as he remembered the blood hound belonging to Albert Mason. Could they be chasing him, he thought. He had to get up and move, and move quickly. He was afraid to turn on the flashlight now. He was thrashing and fighting his way through the underbrush, falling and stumbling his way forward. They were getting closer now and he knew without doubt they were chasing him. God help me he prayed. He knew if those men caught him he would not have a chance out here in the woods alone.

Earl ran blindly now, not knowing or caring if he was still on the logging road. His main purpose was to put as much distance between himself and the sound behind him as he could. Without the flashlight, however, he was fighting a losing battle. Exhausted, Earl made a quick turn to the right. He thought he remembered a creek running at the base of the hill he was following. If he could make it to that creek, maybe the dog would lose his scent.

He had gone only a few yards when he stepped in a hole and felt something snap in his ankle. No God, please no, begged Earl. He had to get to that creek. He felt around on the ground and found a dead tree limb. Testing it to be sure it would support his weight, Earl hobbled down the hillside, sliding halfway down on his backside. They were so close now and Earl wanted to just give up. The thought of Coretta and his boys kept him moving, however. He had to be close to the creek now as he was almost to the base of the hill. Being unfamiliar with his surroundings, Earl stumbled forward and suddenly felt nothing beneath him. He had walked over the edge of the rock wall cut out be the creek below. Had it been in the spring, Earl would have fallen into the water. It had been a dry summer, however, and the creek was now no more than a trickle with small pools collected here and there. Earl hit the rocks below and, mercifully felt no pain as his life slipped away in seconds.

Roscoe was getting excited now, barking and tugging on his leash. The men knew this meant their quarry was near. They could tell where Earl was headed and knew Roscoe might lose the scent if he made it to the creek. Suddenly Roscoe came to a halt and stood looking over the edge of the small cliff. He whined and stood motionless as if unsure what to do. Junior and

Albert shined their lights toward the creek below and saw Earl, lying lifeless on the ground, his feet lying in a small pool of water. His neck was twisted in a grotesque angle and blood was pooling underneath his head.

"We got him boys," said Albert. "He may still be alive. We have to get down there and be sure. If he's not we'll finish the job. Nobody will ever know the difference. He fell Sheriff," said Albert, jokingly.

The men moved a little further down stream and made their way to the creek bed. Earl was indeed dead, they determined. Now what to do with the body? Nobody relished the idea of hauling the body back out of the woods. This decision was made for them as they heard a voice on the ledge above them.

"What have you men done? What did you do to Earl?" yelled Sheriff Martin, making his way down the embankment.

"Let me handle this," said Albert in a low voice.

"Well Sheriff, we decided to take matters into our own hands and give you a little help. We wanted to make sure this murderin nigger didn't get away. Old Roscoe here chased him right to this creek bed. Guess he must have stumbled in the dark and fell," said Albert.

"You men had no business coming out here. I never asked for your help. In fact, I distinctly remember telling you all to go home," Sheriff Martin shouted. He bent to check Earl's pulse and found none.

He rose slowly and glared at the men. "You will all stay right here until daylight at which time I can get a better handle on just what happened. Then you will help lug Earl's body out of here to the main highway where my Deputies are waiting. They can radio for an ambulance to meet us there. In the meantime, I want to hear exactly what happened from the time you left Earl's house," said Sheriff Martin, in a tone no one would dare question.

The men grumbled but made themselves comfortable as they sat down to wait. Sheriff Martin radioed his Deputies and filled them in on what was going on.

"Do you want us to go tell Coretta?" asked one of the Deputies.

"No, that's a job I will need to do myself. I want to know exactly what happened to Earl before I go to see her. Just wait there for the ambulance. We will bring Earl's body out as soon as it gets daylight," Sheriff Martin told the Deputies.

"Now who wants to explain to me what happened here?" asked Sheriff Martin, settling down on a nearby log.

"We knew Old Earl would probably run and we wanted to be sure he didn't get away with killing Sara Mae," said Albert.

"That is my job, not yours or any of the rest of you. Besides, according to Coretta, Earl told her he just stopped by to buy a pint of whisky from Sara Mae. She said he was afraid of being blamed and ran. What I want to know is, how did Earl die?" said Sheriff Martin.

"We didn't lay a hand on him," Junior spoke up. "He must have stumbled off the ledge up there and killed his self. Besides, we know he's the one that done it. The Simpson boys saw him running from the house."

"That doesn't prove him guilty," said Sheriff Martin. "There will be an investigation into what happened to Sara Mae as well as to what happened to Earl. If you boys hadn't been chasing Earl he would probably have stayed on the logging road and never been in this area. There are any number of things you can be charged with and you can bet I am going to see that you are," Sheriff Martin warned.

The sun was beginning to rise in the east and the group could see each other now and make their way around without stumbling over one another. Several of the men got up and made their way behind large trees to relieve their bladder. Sheriff Martin instructed others to gather branches and form a litter to carry Earl's body out to the main road. He did his best to determine what had happened to Earl. The grass, leaves and rocks on the ledge above where Earl lay showed signs of a disturbance. There were leaves and twigs lying under and around Earl's body. The sack of food Coretta had prepared for him lay strewn about on the ground near the body. It looked like Earl had indeed fallen in his rush to get away from the men chasing him. Sheriff Martin would make out his report when he got back to the office. The cause of death would probably be accidental, pending the coroners report.

Sheriff Martin knew he had to notify Coretta of her husband's death, a chore he was not looking forward to. Once Earl's body was loaded into the ambulance, Sheriff Martin instructed all the men to go home with warnings he would be by to see them all again for questioning.

Coretta heard Sheriff Martin's car pull to a stop in front of the house and rushed down the steps to meet him. She came to a halt, however, as she saw the look on his face. He stood at the car a moment, as if to brace himself, then walked towards Coretta.

"What is it Sheriff, did you find my Earl?" asked Coretta, her voice barely above a whisper.

"Lets sit down on the porch Coretta," said Sheriff Martin, as he guided her ahead of him.

"I am afraid I have bad news Coretta. I am so sorry to tell you Earl was killed in an accident last night. He fell off a ledge overlooking Deer Lick Creek and hit his head on the rocks below. I am sure he was running from Albert Mason and that bunch, probably couldn't see in the dark and fell."

Coretta began to wail and rock back and forth. The two boys came running from the house upon hearing their mother and threw themselves into her arms.

"What's wrong Mama?" asked the older of the two. "What's the matter?"

Codetta just gathered the boys to her and kept rocking, the tears streaming down her face.

"I am so sorry Coretta. Those men will be punished for their part in this I promise you that," said Sheriff Martin. "Earl's body was taken to the coroner's office. There will have to be an autopsy due to the circumstances of his death. It will probably be at least three days before Earl's body can be buried. I know you will need to make plans." Sheriff Martin's voice trailed off as he did not know what else he could say to relieve this poor woman's suffering.

Slowly Coretta rose from her chair.   She pushed the boys toward the door and spoke one word to them, "go." They knew from the tone of her voice they should obey and disappeared inside the house. "Those men killed my Earl as sure as the sun will rise in the morning. I heard them say they intended to do just that as they were leaving here. They might not have laid a hand on him, but they were the cause. You know it and I know it. I also know Earl never killed that woman but he will be blamed for it and the person who did it will be walking free. My children will be told their father is a murderer. Life is too hard Sheriff Martin, and I don't know if I care to live in this world anymore." With that, she turned and walked into the house, closing the door on the Sheriff and the cruel world outside.

Sheriff Martin stood in indecision for a moment, not knowing if Coretta should be left alone, due to the last statement she made. He tried to think of someone who might come and be with Coretta to console her. He did not know if she had relatives nearby or friends. This was not unusual as most whites kept to themselves and blacks stayed with their own. He got back in the patrol car and a thought struck him. He remembered Junior bragging that his wife, Lucy, worked with Coretta and implied they were friends. He would drive over there now and see if Lucy could come by and sit with Coretta until her family could be notified.

Junior saw Sheriff Martin's car come to a halt in front of his house and his heart skipped a beat. Why was he here, Junior thought? Surely he could not have found out he was at Sara Mae's yesterday. It was all Junior could do not to rush out the back door and keep on running. He forced himself to answer the door with a warning look at Lucy before he did so.

"Well Sheriff, didn't expect to see you so soon," said Junior, sounding braver than he felt.

"It's Lucy I've come to see," Said Sheriff Martin, as he turned to Lucy.

Junior felt terror like he had never felt before. "What do you need to see her for. She don't know nothin about any of this. Ain't that right Lucy?" Junior asked, in a tone Lucy knew all too well.

"I wanted to ask Lucy if she would mind going over to sit with Coretta for awhile until I can locate some of her family. She's taking Earl's death really badly and I don't think it is good for her to be alone right now. I heard you say she and Lucy were friends and thought she might be of help."

Lucy gasped and sank into a nearby chair, her hands to her face. "What do you mean? What happened to Earl?" Lucy asked, stunned.

"I'm sorry Lucy. I assumed Junior had told you what happened last night. Junior, Albert Mason and that bunch chased Earl through the woods and he fell off a ledge over Deer Lick Creek. We think he hit his head on the rocks when he fell. Coretta is terribly upset, as you can imagine. If you wouldn't mind sitting with her for awhile, I would appreciate it."

"Oh she won't mind will you Lucy?" said Junior, so relieved he was not the reason for the Sheriff's visit.

Lucy rose from her chair, her legs trembling. "I just need to tell Mary to fix some lunch for the children and I will be ready." She started out of the room but turned to look at Sheriff Martin. "Sheriff, are you still looking for the man who killed Sara Mae?"

Junior froze, terror written all over his face. Surely she would not be so stupid as to tell what she knew. He glared at Lucy in warning.

"There will be an investigation Lucy. The Simpson boys saw Earl running from the house but that doesn't make him guilty. Earl can't speak for himself now but I will do my best to determine what happened."

Lucy turned and left the room without another word. She did not know if she could face her friend, knowing what she knew. She could only imagine what Coretta was going through. To have the man she loved accused of murder and then be murdered himself. That's what it was, Lucy thought. If Earl had not died in the accident, those men would have killed him anyway.

Lucy stood for a moment, her back to the room. "I'll be with you in a moment Sheriff," she said then walked out.

Junior breathed a sigh of relief. The moment had passed. If she was going to tell, that was the time.

Lucy was quiet on the ride to Coretta's. She had no idea what she would say to her friend or how she could comfort her. Now, she was a part of this whole mess. She could not chance telling what she knew. Junior had made it clear what he would do to her children.

"I'll be back for you in a little while Lucy, just as soon as I round up some of her family," said Sheriff Martin.

Lucy turned and walked slowly toward the house. The house was silent as she stepped upon the porch.

Hesitantly, Lucy knocked on the door and called out, "Coretta, it's me, Lucy."

Lucy began to think no one was coming to the door when she heard footsteps from inside. Coretta opened the door and fell into Lucy's arms, her whole body shaking. Lucy guided her back inside and to the nearest bed. They sat holding each other, rocking back and forth, each sobbing for different reasons. Coretta, for the loss of her husband and Lucy, for the guilt she felt over her part in this woman's misery. She knew if she had told someone what she knew about Junior, Earl would probably still be alive. She and her children might be dead, but Earl would still be alive.

Coretta's two children had been sitting quietly on the floor, a look of confusion and bewilderment on their little faces. Lucy knew from her own experiences, children are resilient and Coretta's children were no exception. They would be all right but she knew Coretta's life would never be the same.

Exhausted, Coretta patted Lucy's hand and rose to prepare lunch for her children. She had completely forgotten about breakfast. They must be starved she thought. As Coretta prepared lunch, she and Lucy talked about the funeral preparations and what Coretta might do now that her husband was gone.

"I know they won't look any further for who ever killed that woman," said Codetta. "Earl is dead and can't speak for himself. He is a black man, and we both know it will be easy for everyone to just assume he did it and go on. I appreciate our friendship Lucy, and you have never made me feel uncomfortable about the difference in our color. I am glad I got to know you. Maybe if there were more people like you and Sheriff Martin out there, this would be a better world."

Lucy felt like she would scream if they did not speak of something else. "What do you think you will do, Coretta? Will you stay here in this house and keep working? Do you have family here who can help you?" she asked, hoping Coretta could not see how uncomfortable she was.

"I have a second cousin who lives over on Tunnel Road. We are not close but I am sure she and her family would take us in if necessary. Earl has several family members who live in this area and they'll help out I'm sure. Most of my family lives in Detroit. They moved there to work in the automotive factories. They are doing quite well and blacks are treated better in the north. There is more opportunity there. Nothing here but back breaking work in the fields or sawmills like Earl. I may just pack up my children and head up that way," Coretta said tiredly.

"I am sorry Coretta, for everything. I cherish our friendship and it pains me to think of you leaving, but I understand. I don't know if I ever told you, but you are the first and only friend I ever had. I will miss you something awful if you go," said Lucy, bursting into tears.

Now it was Coretta's turn to comfort Lucy. She knew what a hard life Lucy had and knew that her husband was cruel to her and their children. "Lucy, why don't you leave that no good man? You have a job and can support yourself now. There's no reason to stay with someone who is so mean to you. I've seen the bruises and I am sure that's just a small part of the abuse," Coretta said, hoping she was not overstepping her bounds.

"Oh Coretta, if it were only that simple," sighed Lucy. "Junior would kill us all before he would let us leave. Lord knows he has told me often enough what he would do. He is the devil himself and I hate him for what he has done to our children. Thank God they will all be grown up in a few years and never have to be around him again."

"I guess we all have our crosses to bear. It's so easy to say what you would or would not do when you have never walked in that person's shoes. If there was anything at all I could do to help you Lucy, you know I would," said Coretta.

"I know Coretta, I know," said Lucy, and the two women embraced, each knowing their time together was coming to an end soon.

Sheriff Martin returned later in the afternoon with one of Earl's sisters. She was a large commanding woman who took Coretta into her arms and assured her everything was going to be all right. Lucy knew she was in good hands, so gave her one last hug and left with Sheriff Martin.

"What will happen now Sheriff Martin?" asked Lucy. "Will anything be done to Junior and all those men who chased Earl last night?"

"We will wait for the autopsy reports from both Sara Mae and Earl. If they can pinpoint the time of death for Sara Mae, we might be able to tell if Earl was there within the time frame of her murder. If he wasn't, then we'll have to keep looking for the responsible person," said Sheriff Martin.

"And Junior, what will happen to him for his part in this?" Lucy asked again, hoping he would be taken to jail.

"I can't say right now Lucy. The least will be a charge of interfering with an investigation and tampering with evidence at the crime scene. Those men destroyed any evidence there might have been at Sara Maes.

Lucy got out of the patrol car and slowly made her way to the house, not sure what mood Junior would be in and what horror awaited her there.

"It's about time you got back," said Junior, grabbing Lucy by the hair and slapping her hard across the face. "Thought you were smart with that little stunt you pulled with the Sheriff didn't you. Well just in case you have any doubts about what I said, you might want to take a look in the back room," said Junior and gave Lucy a shove in that direction.

The lighting in the room was dim as there was only one window and it was partially shaded by a bush growing up the outside wall. Lucy heard a whimper and turned in the direction of the sound, a feeling of dread enveloping her. There in the corner, lay her youngest child, Glory. She was only ten and small for her age. Glory was lying in the fetal position with her thumb in her mouth. Lucy gently raised her to the sitting position and gasped at what she saw. Glory's face was swollen and blood had dried under her nose and around her mouth. One of her lips protruded grotesquely and upon checking closer, Lucy could see a gash on the inside of her lip. She knew there would be further injuries but this was enough to throw her into a fury. She rose with Glory in her arms and went to face Junior.

"What kind of man are you?" asked Lucy, through gritted teeth. "How could you do this to your own child? She did nothing to deserve this and I won't let you get away with it. I've had enough Junior. I want you to leave this house and never come back."

Junior looked at Lucy as if she had lost her mind, then began to laugh. "I won't be going anywhere woman. I told you not to mess with me. Now put her to bed and get some supper started. That's just a sample of what I will do if you give me any more trouble," hissed Junior.

Lucy could feel her courage slipping. She hated herself almost as much as she hated Junior. Her only hope was that Junior would be found out and put in jail where he could not get at her and the children.

There are laws to protect women and children now for this type of treatment but during Lucy's time there was very little done to protect the innocent. Families in rural communities were pretty much left alone to discipline their children however the saw fit. "Spare the rod and spoil the child" was a favorite saying of most.

CHAPTER 24

Days passed and no one was arrested for Sara Mae's death. Junior and Albert Mason's bunch were fined and put on six months probation for their interference. Earl's death was ruled accidental and things returned to normal. Lucy returned to work with Coretta but could not look her friend in the eye. Coretta knew something had changed between them but couldn't figure out just what it was. Lucy was her normal sweet self but something was different, and Coretta felt it.

Several weeks had passed when Coretta came to work one day and announced she and her boys would be moving away. She was taking her children and moving to Michigan with her relatives. There was the promise of a job waiting for her and she saw no reason to stay. Although it was never officially declared that Earl murdered Sara Mae, everyone assumed he had. Coretta stayed home as much as possible but had to go grocery shopping at least once a week. If Junior or some of his friends happened to be in the store, Coretta was taunted and mocked until she could stand it no longer. Thank God, her children were still in the all black school. She could only imagine what it would be like for them in the white school. It looked like that might be a possibility in the very near future and she wanted no part of it.

Lucy was devastated at Coretta's news but at the same time, she was relieved. The guilt was eating her alive. She had lost weight and jumped at the least unexpected noise. She would miss her friend terribly but knew in her heart it was the best for Coretta and her children.

On the day Coretta left, Lucy asked her supervisor if she could take her lunch time early. She walked the short distance to the bus stop and saw her friend off. I'll write, promised Coretta, as did Lucy, both knowing they probably never would. There was just too much pain in keeping the friendship alive.

CHAPTER 25

The years slipped by and most people forgot about Earl and Sara Mae. When the subject was brought up now it was "remember when Old Earl killed Sara Mae and then fell and broke his own neck." Lucy continued to work, with Junior there every payday for his cut. He had long since stopped picking her up except on payday. Then, he was Johnny on the spot. Lucy's knees and back ached after working all day. The walk home was torture but, as always, she did what she had to do.

The children were all gone now, the youngest having graduated just two months earlier. They would drop by occasionally to see Lucy but didn't stay long. Lucy had managed to get all twelve of her children through high school. They had all gone on to have successful lives. There were two teachers, a nurse, an engineer and one daughter, Emma, who worked for the government. One day Emma came by to pick her mother up when she got off from work.

"What a nice surprise," said Lucy, climbing into Emma's sleek new car. Lucy was so proud of her children's success, but was to shy to tell them so.

"Mama, I want to talk to you about something," said Emma. She wanted to talk to her mother without Junior around. "Me, Sunny and some of the other kid's talked about this and decided we needed to do something to make your life a little easier," said Emma, as she pulled the car into a vacant lot near the meat packing plant. "We bought this lot for you Mama. You will be eligible for Social Security in a few more years. You won't have to work anymore then, Mama. Until then, we want to make a good down payment on a new house for you right here on this lot. You will be really close to work and your payments will be so small you can still quit work when you get old enough for your Social Security. Just think about it Mama, you will have running water and a bathroom in the house for the first time. Sunny says he will buy you a washing machine and maybe even a TV. If you ever have trouble making the payments we will all chip in and help. I can get the loan approved where I work," Emma rattled on, hardly able to contain her excitement.

She looked over at Lucy and was surprised to see her mother with tears rolling down her cheeks. "Mama, I didn't mean to upset you. We would make the payments ourselves but we know how prideful you are. This is something we all want to do, in return for all you've done for us."

Lucy could hardly speak, her emotions were so strong. "I don't deserve it Emma," she whispered. "After what you had to go through with your Daddy, I don't deserve it."

"That was him Mama. We never blamed you. Don't you know we saw the beatings you took for us and the sacrifices you made to keep us in school? Mama, this is something we all want to do. It would make us so happy if you would accept this gift from us. Lonnie says he can start on the house next week and be done within two months, if you say it is what you want," said Emma, hopefully. Lonnie was a very much in demand contractor and the husband of Lucy's daughter, Janie.

"What about your father Emma?" asked Lucy, reluctantly. "Where does he fit into this picture?"

"That is up to you Mama. I would like to say, leave him behind, but it is not my place to tell you that. You will have to make that decision and we will all abide by it. You know we would all visit you more if he wasn't there. But again, I don't want to influence your decision," Emma finished, looking at her Mother hopefully.

"I don't know if I will have the courage to stand up to your Daddy. It seems pointless at this point. He pretty much leaves me alone now. Since you children are gone, he has nothing to hold over me anymore. He comes and goes as he pleases and takes money from me, but other than that, we hardly say a word to each other."

"Oh Mama, I am so sorry for all you have had to go through," said Emma, taking her Mother's hand. "You do what ever you want with regards to Daddy, but we would all be happy knowing you are living in some comfort for the first time in your life."

"All right then, if you are sure I can afford it," said Lucy, beginning to feel more excitement than she had felt in years.

It was decided Lonnie and his crew would start on the house in two weeks. Emma pulled out the plans and showed them to Lucy. It would be a small house, two bedrooms, a living room, kitchen with a bar and small eating area to one side. There would be a laundry room and bathroom with hardwood and tile on the floors. There was a small front porch and a back porch where Lucy could sit in the evenings.

"Sunny, Jesse and Jennie want to buy you some new furniture too Mama. That old stuff you've been hauling around for years is a mess and hardly worth moving. Oh it will be so wonderful Mama. Just think of it, you will be cool in the summer and warm in the winter. No more cutting wood for the fireplace," said Emma, bubbling with excitement.

"I won't know what to do with myself, Emma. You will have to come and show me how to operate everything," said Lucy. The two of them giggled and planned all the way home.

Lucy didn't know what she was going to do about Junior. Should she tell him about the house or just up and move away. She giggled at the prospect. Boy, old Junior would not see that one coming, she thought. She could hardly sleep she was so excited. She decided to wait awhile before telling Junior about the house. She didn't know why, although deep down, she knew it was because she dreaded confronting him. In the end, she decided it was hardly worth it. She did not have that many years left. Her children were not around for him to hurt anymore. He no longer beat her. In fact he pretty much ignored her, which was fine with Lucy.

For some reason, Lucy kept putting off discussing the matter of the house with Junior. She just didn't know what she wanted to do or how to bring the subject up. The matter settled itself one day when Junior came home and asked Lucy if she knew who was building the house next to the meat processing plant.

She sighed and sat down at the table across from Junior. She guessed she might as well get it over with, she thought. "As a matter of fact I do Junior. It is my house. Emma and the kids are helping me get the house. They bought the lot and made the down payment on the house. Emma says the payments will be something I can handle and if necessary, they can help out if need be."

Junior sat stunned at this bit of news. "Why didn't you tell me about this?" asked Junior, totally confused. He had always had the upper hand and control over Lucy most of their married lives. This news threw him totally off guard.

"To tell you the truth Junior, I have been trying to decide whether to leave you behind to fend for yourself. It is what the kids want, you know. You were a terrible father Junior. All those years of abuse from you left their mark. Why do you think they hardly ever come around? You know that old saying, "you reap what you sew," well it's your reaping time, Junior."

Junior jumped to his feet, his chair hitting the floor behind him. He reached across the table and grabbed Lucy by the hair, his fist raised as if to strike. Something about the look in Lucy's eye's held him in that position for several seconds before he let go, pushing Lucy back into her chair. He stood panting, not sure what to do. He was suddenly terrified at the thought of Lucy leaving him. Who would take care of him, he thought. He was too old to start work now. Slowly, Junior righted his chair and sat across from Lucy, his head bowed.

"Don't worry Junior. I am not leaving you behind, even though I know I should. Don't get me wrong, I care nothing for you Junior, but I am a compassionate person. I know you would be homeless if I left you here. There will be certain conditions, however. You will never touch me again, in any way, shape or form. I will tolerate no verbal abuse. You can live there with me as long as you treat me with respect and clean up after yourself. I will no longer be waiting on you hand and foot, so don't expect it. I know you will need a few dollars now and then but it will be just that, a few dollars. If you want more you will need to take a job and earn it. Do we understand each other?" Lucy finished.

Junior mumbled, "yeah" so low Lucy could hardly hear him, and with that, got up and left the room.

CHAPTER 26

On the day Lucy moved into her new house, she was delirious with excitement. All the children came and moved in the new furniture. The girls sewed curtains and hung them on the windows. They laughed until they cried at Lucy's excitement as she flushed the commode for the first time. Junior stood off to the side and sulked. The children all ignored him and vowed not to let him spoil this for their mother. They had hoped she would leave Junior behind, but respected her decision.

Lucy walked around on cloud nine for days. She scrubbed and cleaned the house so often the children feared she would wear the finish off the floor. Her life was so much easier now. She hardly noticed the pain in her knees as she walked to and from work. Junior came and went with hardly a word. The tension in the house was unbearable at times. Lucy knew he hated her because he no longer had the upper hand.

At times she felt the guilt descend upon her about Coretta and she could feel herself slipping back into that old despair. She had learned to put it out of her mind by cleaning and thinking of her children until one day it all came crashing back.

She had just gotten off work and was starting the walk home when she was approached by a young black man. He was well dressed and didn't seem to have any ill intentions.

"Good evening Miss Lucy," said the young man, his cap in hand. "I know you don't remember me but you used to work with my Mama, Coretta."

"My word, is this little Sampson, or is it Henry?" exclaimed Lucy, in shock.

"It's Sampson, Maam. I came to see you because Mama is ill and we don't expect to have her with us much longer. Mama never got over what happened to my Pappy. She speaks of you often, and what a good woman and friend you were to her. She said you knew about what happened to my Pappy, Ms. Lucy," the young man said nervously.

Lucy stood for a moment, not sure how to respond. She wasn't sure exactly what Sampson meant by his last comment. "Oh Sampson, I am so sorry to hear about your mother. She was the first and only friend I ever had. We had such wonderful talks while we went about working. It made the day go by much faster. Goodness Sampson, let's go on up to the house and sit on the porch while we talk. I'll fix us a nice glass of lemonade. I live right up there in that little white house," said Lucy, proudly pointing to her new home.

They were comfortably seated on the porch, Sampson on the swing and Lucy in her favorite rocker. They sat talking about the old days when Lucy and Coretta had worked together, Lucy telling Sampson some of her favorite memories of their friendship. She knew she was avoiding the lingering question of what happened to Sampson's father. She knew Sampson would not let it go, however, and he didn't.

"Miss Lucy, I don't mean to press you, but I would really like to know about my father. I don't remember a lot about the night he died except how Mama cried for so long and you and the Sheriff came to see us. Mama never really told us what happened. We asked her when we got older but she just said it was best we didn't know."

Lucy took a long drink of her lemonade, trying to gather her thoughts. "Sampson, your daddy was a good man. I know that from all the things your mother told me about him. I know he loved your mother and you boys a lot. On the same day your daddy died, there was another death, a woman of, let's just say question-able character. She had men visitors and sold whiskey from her house. It seems your daddy went by there to get a bottle of whiskey. It was Friday and Coretta said Earl liked to get a pint of whiskey to relax after a hard weeks work. Earl told your mother Sara Mae was already dead when he got there. Two boys happened to drive by just as Earl was coming out of the house. He panicked and ran into the woods."

Lucy had to stop for a moment to gather her thoughts. That terrible nightmare was all coming back to her and she could feel herself slipping back in time. "A group of men calling themselves the "Militia" chased him through the woods after he left your house that night. I know you don't remember what it was like back then Sampson, so it may be hard for you to understand. Earl knew he would probably be charged with Sara Mae's murder, even though he had nothing to do with it, so he decided to leave the county in hopes the real murderer would be caught. It was his plan to go to his brother's house and lay low until he could return to you kids and your mother. One of those men owned a blood hound and they chased Earl through those woods in the dark. According to the Sheriff, he stumbled off an embankment in the dark, falling into a dry creek bed below. The fall broke his neck and crushed his skull. The Sheriff said the autopsy showed he died almost instantly and felt no pain," Lucy finished.

"What happened to those men, Miss Lucy? It seems like they were responsible for my father's death in some way," said Sampson.

"Oh, they were fined and put on probation, but that's about it," said Lucy, failing to mention that her own husband had been part of the group. It appeared that Sampson wasn't aware of that fact, and Lucy wondered why Coretta had not mentioned it to her children.

Lucy was debating on just what to tell Sampson when she saw Junior pull his old truck into the driveway. She did not know how he would react at seeing her sitting on the porch with a young black man. Junior was still as big a racist as he had ever been and Lucy knew he would never change. She braced herself for a confrontation but was determined to stand her ground. Sampson was her guest, in her home.

"What's he doing here," asked Junior. "What you want boy?" he asked as he came up on the porch.

"This is Sampson, Coretta's oldest boy," said Lucy. He stopped by to tell me his mother is ill and wanted some details about what happened to his father," Lucy said, staring Junior down. She knew the last remark would catch him off guard. Junior and Lucy never spoke of that night but it was there, all the time. The terrible secret they shared.

Junior gave Sampson a hard look then went inside, slamming the door behind him.

"I'm sorry Miss Lucy. I don't want to cause any trouble," said Sampson. He was all to aware that people like Junior still existed. "Maybe I had best go. I appreciate you taking the time to talk to me. I'm staying over at Uncle Herman's for a few days and I will try to stop by to see you again before I go back home if it is all right," Sampson said, rising to leave.

"I'm sorry Sampson, for Junior's behavior. You stop by any time. I don't work on the weekends and I am here every evening after work. I would love to see Coretta again. She was a dear person and I missed her terribly when you all moved away," Lucy said, hoping Junior's rudeness would not prevent Sampson from visiting her again.

"I'll do that Miss Lucy." Sampson started down the walk, then turned around, as an idea struck him. "Miss Lucy why don't you come visit Mama? It would be such a wonderful surprise for her. The bus ride is about eight hours and I could meet you at the station."

"Oh, I don't know Sampson. As much as I would love to see your mother, I have never been out of this county. I would be terrified to ride the bus that far away by myself," said Lucy. Seeing the look of disappointment on Sampson's face, Lucy promised she would give it some serious thought and asked Sampson to leave his address and phone number before he left town.

Sampson came by a few days later after Lucy had gotten off work. Junior wasn't home and Lucy was grateful. She and Sampson had a nice chat and Sampson gave Lucy his address and phone number before leaving. Lucy stuck it away in her purse, never thinking she would use it.

CHAPTER 27

For weeks after Sampson's visit Lucy could not get him off her mind. The old guilt was back and she was struggling to ward off the depression. She could hardly stand to look at Junior, and at times, wished she had left him behind. It would have been easier than getting him out of the house now. There was something desperate about Junior at times, and the old fear Lucy had lived with so long had returned.

Lucy found herself going to bed earlier and earlier. She had to force herself to get up in the mornings. Sunny and Emma had come by to visit one Saturday and found Lucy still in bed. This was so unlike their Mother and they were getting worried. They couldn't understand what was bothering her. Other than having to work, her life was easier now than at any other time. Sunny and Emma talked later and agreed they had to keep a close eye on their mother. If this continued they might need to get her to a doctor.

As had become her habit, Lucy went to bed early and had fallen into a restless sleep when she was awakened by a noise outside her window. She lay listening for a moment and realized it was her little dog, Tiger. He was whining softly just below the window sill. Tiger had shown up at Lucy's house one day and lay trembling on the ground as she approached him. Lucy saw in the dog something of herself so she fed and petted him until the trembling of his little body stopped. He was Lucy's dog from that moment.

Lucy got out of bed and made her way to the window. A full moon cast an eerie light over the landscape of the yard. A movement caught her eye near the small rose bush she had planted a few days before. She squinted her eyes and realized the thing moving about on the ground was Junior.

Junior had left the house late that afternoon without a word to Lucy. She knew he would probably be heading to the nearby "beer joint" as the locals called it. It was no more than a shack hidden back in the woods off the main road. Lucy knew a lot of questionable activities went on there but did not care that Junior chose to spend his time there. It took him out of the house and away from her.

Lucy rose and went to the front of the house where she could get a better view. She could hear Junior's voice now but could not make out the garbled sounds. She was sure he was trying to call out to her but made no move in his direction.

Junior had been having dizzy spells lately and had finally gone to the county nurse. He was told he had dangerously high blood pressure and was given a prescription for medication. Junior just tossed it away. "He had better things to spend his money on," he had told Lucy. He was thrashing about wildly now, but still, Lucy could not move. She knew the thing he had been warned about had happened. The nurse had told Junior he could have a stroke if he failed to take his medication.

Lucy knew she should do the humane thing and help him but she could not make herself move. She pulled up her rocker and sat in front of the window, watching her husband as if in a trance. All the years of neglect, abuse and torture held her in that chair. She sat there in the dim moonlight and though back to when it all started so many years before.

The first rays of sunlight peeked over the tree tops and Lucy jerked awake. She must have dozed off. Why was she sitting in the rocker? Then it all came rushing back. Junior, he had been lying in the yard, she thought, as she rose from her chair and rushed outside. She didn't hear him now but saw him lying in the ditch at the front of the yard. She had to do something before her grandchildren started arriving. Jesse and Clara lived nearby and their children liked to catch the school bus in front of Lucy's house. They loved sitting on the front porch eating their Grandmother's warm biscuits and jelly while waiting for the bus. There would be no biscuits and jelly on this day, however.

Lucy went to where Junior lay and bent down to check on him. She was almost sure he was dead but checked his pulse. Finding none, she rose and made her way back to the house. She felt no sorrow at Junior's passing. A fleeting surge of guilt passed quickly as she remembered she failed to do anything to help him.

Sunny had insisted on having a telephone installed for his mother, even though she seldom used it. Several of the children chipped in and paid the bill for her. The phone was as much for their peace of mind as it was for Lucy. Today, she was grateful for the phone. Not knowing what else to do, Lucy called Jesse and Clara and explained what had happened. She told them they should not let the kids come today and asked Jesse what she should do about Junior.

"Call the Sheriff, Mama, and I will be right there," Jesse told her. He too felt no grief at his father's passing. It was a terrible thing, he thought, but it was true.

Lucy made her call, then took a quilt down to where Junior lay and covered the body. She went back to the house, sat in her rocker and waited.

Just as Lucy suspected, it was determined that Junior did have a stroke. He was buried in the cemetery next to his mother and father. Lucy had already reserved her spot next to the body of her mother. Newcomers to the area thought it strange that Lucy and Junior would not be buried side by side after all those years together. Those who knew them, however, understood completely.

All the children and grandchildren attended the funeral along with some of the older people of the community. Most of Junior's family were either dead or had moved away and could not be there. For Lucy and her children it was more about closure. It was like a new beginning for all of them.

A week went by with little sleep for Lucy. She could think of nothing else but poor Coretta and her boys. The poor woman would die not knowing for sure if her husband was a murderer. Lucy knew Coretta felt in her heart Earl was innocent but there would always be that doubt for her sons.

Lucy thought the whole thing through and finally came to a decision. Junior was dead and could no longer hurt her or the children. She was the only one who could set things right for Coretta and her children. She had to clear Earl's name even though it would mean telling the world that her husband, and the father of her children, was a murderer.

She had to let all the kids know of her plans. If they objected, she wasn't sure what she would do. They had been hurt so much in their life at Junior's hand, this would be one more thing. At the same time, she knew she could no longer live with the guilt. She did not know what would happen to her. She didn't know if she could be punished for her silence all these years. She picked up the phone and started calling.

She didn't tell any of the children what she wanted, only that it was important. They all assumed it had to do with their father's death. Two of the children lived in Memphis and could not get there until the weekend so it was decided they would all meet at Lucy's house on Saturday, two days later.

Saturday morning came and Lucy was up bright and early, so nervous she could not eat. She fed Tiger, put him outside, and sat down to wait. By noon all the children had arrived. They sat around the living room, anxiously awaiting their Mothers explanation as to why she had summoned them all.

Lucy served them all lemonade and took a seat in her rocker. She looked around the room at her children's expectant faces and her heart burst with pride and love for them. She sighed, opened her mouth to speak, but nothing came out. She started again but still could not get the words out. She bowed her head and started sobbing, her whole body shaking. The family all looked at each other in shock. Surely it couldn't be grief over the loss of Junior, they thought. Sunny and Emma rushed to their mother's side and knelt on the floor beside her.

"Mama, whatever is the matter?" asked Emma, taking her mother's hand.

Lucy raised her head and accepted the handkerchief from Sunny. Wiping her eyes, she took a deep breath and started again. "I have something to tell all of you, and I don't know quite how to do it. I hope and pray it doesn't cause any of you pain but it's something I can no longer live with," said Lucy, placing her hand on

Emma's head as her daughter settled herself on the floor beside her.

"Some of you are too young to remember much about this, but Sunny, I know you, Jesse, Jennie and Emma will remember. And you Glory, you were only ten at the time, but I'm sure it will come back to you when I explain. Year's ago a woman was killed, beaten to death, they said. You remember Sunny, Sara Mae Johnson. If you recall, Coretta's husband, Earl, was thought to be the one who did it. He died the same night. Some men, including your father, chased him through the woods and he fell off an embankment into a dry creek bed, breaking his neck," Lucy said, pausing to catch her breath.

"I remember all about that Mama," said Sunny. "But what does all that have to do with us?"

Lucy felt the tears coming again and took a deep breath to gain control. She had started this and knew she had to finish.

"Earl wasn't the one who killed that woman. It was your father," said Lucy. There was a collective gasp from everyone in the room. They knew their father was a brutal, cruel man but this was something they had never imagined.

"My God, Mama, how do you know this?" asked Jesse. He knew his mother and knew she would not make such an accusation unless it was true.

"The afternoon Sara Mae was killed, your father came home all out of breath, with blood on his face and clothes. He had scratch marks all over his arms. His ear was bruised and if you looked closely, you could see it was teeth marks. He pulled his clothes off and went outside without a stitch on, he was in such a hurry, built a fire under the wash pot and burned all his clothes. When I asked him about it, he threatened me and told me I was to tell anyone who came asking, that he had been at home all evening. When I told him I wouldn't lie for him, he told me he would kill one of you children. You can imagine how terrified I was. I could take the beatings from him but I had to protect you kid's. I believed what he said and, God help me, when the Sheriff came by I lied," Lucy finished, bursting into tears again.

"Mama, we know you did what you thought you had to do," said Sunny, remembering the blows he had taken from his father.

Lucy dried her eyes again and went on. "The Sheriff came by and asked me if I would go over and stay with Coretta until he could find some of their relatives. You can imagine how I felt, facing the only friend I ever had, knowing what I knew but being unable to tell. When I got back home, Junior was waiting for me. He was so afraid I would tell the Sheriff something I guess he felt like he needed to make a believer of me. First he beat me, then proudly told me to take a look at "Mama's pet" in the next room. That's where I found you Glory, curled up in the corner where he left you.

He had beaten you senseless then tossed you in the corner like a piece of trash."

By now everyone in the room was crying, all the years of abuse coming back. Glory threw herself at her mother's feet and rested her face in her mother's lap, sobbing.

"I could never understand Mama, why he did that. Usually when he hit us it was because we had done something to make him mad. I was sitting in the bedroom just cutting out paper dolls. I was so afraid Mama. Sometimes I still have nightmares about that night."

"I'm so sorry Glory, sorry for all of you. Sorry I couldn't do more to protect you. Guess I was just so beaten down by then and so afraid for all of you," said Lucy. "But now that I have told you this dirty little secret, I want to know how you would feel about my telling the Sheriff what I know. Sampson, Coretta's oldest son came by a few weeks ago and said his mother was ill and not expected to live long. He was asking questions about what happened to his father. Seems Coretta never discussed it with her children. I want your permission to clear Earl's name and go see Coretta before she dies. She and her children deserve that, Lucy finished, looking at her children closely.

"That means everyone would have to know Daddy was the real killer, said Lanny, the youngest of the bunch.

"Everyone around here who knew Daddy knows what a horrible person he was," said Emma. "I don't think anyone will be surprised. It will be the talk of the town for awhile that's for sure, but that poor woman and her children have the right to know."

"Is that what's been bothering you so much all these years Mama?" asked Sunny. "We have been so worried about you. If you had just told us, maybe we could have done something to help you."

"I was still afraid of what Junior would do Sunny. He didn't have you children in the house anymore but every once in awhile he would feel the need to remind me what he could do if I ever told. Have you never wondered why I didn't want the grandkid's to spend the night? There was always the threat, but Junior is gone now and he can't hurt anyone again. Now I need to know how you all feel about this," said Lucy, almost pleading for understanding.

"I know it will be rough on all our kid's for awhile, you know, the teasing at school and all," said Jesse. I imagine it will be nothing compared to what Coretta and her children went through at the time," said Jesse, thoughtfully.

"What about you Mama?" Have you thought about what might happen to you for not telling what you knew?" asked Sunny, always the cautious one.

"I've thought about it and truth is, I don't really know. I'm just not sure I can go on living with this guilt anymore. If you children want the secret kept, guess I will have to go on, same as always but I hope you agree with me, it has to be told."

The children discussed the situation among themselves for awhile as Lucy prepared sandwiches for lunch. The younger children, having escaped the worst of their father's brutality were leaning towards keeping the secret. They did not remember Coretta and her children and, somewhat selfishly, thought only of how the gossip would affect them. They were finally won over, however, when the other children pointed out what the guilt was doing to their mother.

"Mama, we have all agreed. You have to tell the authorities what you know. We don't think they will do anything to you because you were afraid for you life and our lives as well. Anyone who knew Daddy knows what he was capable of. We think it would be wiser to call Harry Martin instead of Sheriff Mills. Mr. Martin was Sheriff then and is familiar with the case. If you agree, we will call Mr. Martin and see if he can come over this afternoon while we are all here," Sunny finished, seeing the relieved look in his mother's eyes.

CHAPTER 28

Harry Martin had just gotten out of the shower when his wife called him to the phone. "Mr. Martin, this is Sunny McGregor. How have you been?" asked Sunny, not quite sure what to say.

"Just fine Sunny. What can I do for your?" asked Mr. Martin, a bit puzzled.

"All us kid's are here at Mama's house and were wondering if you might be free to come over this afternoon while we are all here together. Mama has something she needs to talk to you about and it's very important, if you can find the time," Sunny finished.

"Well I can't see any reason why not Sunny. I don't have any plans for the evening. Can you give me an idea what this is about?" asked Mr. Martin, his curiosity aroused.

"It's about the murder case you worked on back when you were Sheriff. You remember, Sara Mae Johnson," said Sunny, not wanting to get into it all on the phone.

"I'll be there within an hour," said Mr. Martin, feeling a stir of excitement. He had always had a bad feeling about that case. He had not believed Earl was the guilty person even though what little evidence they had pointed in his direction.

The emotional stress was taking a toll on all of them, especially Lucy. By the time Harry Martin arrived, they were all exhausted and ready to get this terrible thing over with.

Sunny met Mr. Martin at the door and led him to a chair beside Lucy. After being served with a glass of lemonade by Emma, he turned to Lucy and said, "What's all this about Lucy?"

"Sheriff," Lucy started nervously. "I'm sorry, I know you are not the sheriff anymore but I feel more comfortable calling you that, if it is all right."

"That's fine Lucy, what ever you feel comfortable with. Sunny tells me you wanted to tell me something about Sara Mae Johnson's murder case."

"Yes, I have lived with this all these years Sheriff Martin. Now that Junior is gone, I have no reason to be afraid anymore. Earl didn't kill Sara Mae, Sheriff, Junior did," said Lucy, feeling a load lift from her shoulders.

"How do you know this Lucy?" asked Harry Martin, so excited he could hardly contain himself.

"He told me so. Not at first mind you, but he came right out and admitted it later. The day Sara Mae was killed Junior came home with his arms all scratched up and his ear had a big bruise. If you looked at it closely you could see the teeth marks. He wore a long sleeved shirt around for days and told people he had bumped his ear on the door frame. Anyway, when he came home that day, he stripped off his clothes and burned them under the wash pot. He told me if anyone came asking questions, I was to tell them he had been home all evening. When I told him I wouldn't lie, he beat me and told me he would kill one of the kids if I didn't do what he wanted," said Lucy, staring ahead, reliving the moment as though it were yesterday.

"Lucy, why didn't you tell me then? I would have arrested him and he couldn't have hurt you or the kids," said Harry Martin.

"You remember taking me over to stay with Coretta that evening Sheriff? While I was gone Junior beat Glory there something terrible, just as a warning to me as to what he would do if I dared tell anyone. She was only ten at the time. You should have seen her, all curled into a little ball in the corner, sucking her thumb," said Lucy, the tears streaming down her face now.

Glory sat with her face in her hands sobbing as well. Of all the children, this was probably most painful for her, Lucy thought.

"Oh Lucy, I had heard stories of Junior and how he treated you and the children, but I had no idea. You know they have laws against that kind of abuse, Lucy," said Mr. Martin, leaning forward, his elbows resting on his knees.

"And then what Sheriff, What do you think Junior would have done when he got out of jail?" asked Lucy. "Don't you think I thought of that? I thought of everything. Why, while I am confessing, I may as well tell you this. One day after a particularly bad time with Junior, I was putting out rat poison in the corn crib. It suddenly came to me that just a little bit of that poison could end it all. I fed it to him that night in some cabbage," said Lucy, near hysteria now.

There was a collective gasp from everyone in the room. "Mama, what are you saying?" asked Sonny.

"Oh, as you know, he didn't die as I had hoped. He just got an upset stomach and had to run to the outhouse about fifty times," Lucy said, and started to giggle, then the sobs came.

This time there was no stopping. The sobbing and laughter went on for several minutes before Emma came and gathered her mother into her arms, trying to console her.

"She's hysterical," said Mr. Martin. "Do any of you have something that might settle her nerves? I'm afraid all this has been too much for her, poor woman. With all that she has lived through, it's a miracle she still has her sanity."

"I have my sleeping medicine," offered Clara, handing the bottle to Emma.

"That might be best for now," said Sunny, helping his mother from her chair and leading her, still sobbing, to her bedroom.

Emma coaxed her mother into taking the medicine while Clara removed her shoes and covered her with a blanket. "Rest for awhile now Mama, some of us will stay the night and we can finish this tomorrow when you are feeling better."

Lucy was so exhausted she could do no more than nod. In a matter of minutes, she was sound asleep.

"What will happen now Mr. Martin?" asked Sunny, as the others listened with concern.

"Well, the case will be reopened and when Lucy is feeling better, I'll get Sheriff Mills to come out for her statement. It will only be a formality. Since Junior and Earl are both dead, they will simply take Lucy's statement, change the records to show Junior as the guilty party and close the case."

"What about Mama?" Emma asked. "Will anything be done to her for not telling what she knew back then?"

"I will talk to Sheriff Mills and explain her situation. She did what she had to. It was to protect herself and her children. As for the matter of the rat poison, that will be our little secret. There will probably be a little talk about the murder, you know how small communities are, but I think, after what your mother has been through, that will be minor," said Mr. Martin, rising to go.

"Mama is planning to go see Coretta and tell her everything," said Emma. "I think it will be good for Mama and Coretta to finally get this behind them. Earl's children deserve to know their father was not a murderer."

"Your mother is a very brave woman. You kid's are lucky to have her for a mother," said Mr. Martin, as he walked out onto the porch. "I'll bring Sheriff Mills out to see your mother tomorrow if she is up to it. I assume one of you will be staying the night so I'll call before we come."

It was decided that Emma and Glory would stay with Lucy as neither of them had children to care for. Jesse would go home, but be close by if needed. Several of the children wanted to be there the next day when Lucy gave her statement and promised to return as they left.

Before giving her statement the next day, Lucy made the Sheriff promise not to tell anyone until she could go see Coretta. "I promise I will go the first part of this week if I can get in touch with Sampson. That's

Coretta's oldest son," said Lucy, not sure Sheriff Mills would remember.

"I don't guess it makes a lot of difference after all this time. A few more days won't hurt. Lord knows, that poor woman deserves a little consideration," said Sheriff Mills, shaking his head sadly. He and Mr. Martin left, glad this case could finally be solved and a man's record cleared.

CHAPTER 29

Over Lucy's protests, it was decided Emma would drive Lucy up to see Coretta the next day. Lucy insisted she could ride the bus but Emma would hear nothing of it. She knew this was going to be a stressful trip for her mother and wanted to be there with her.

The call was made to Sampson who was jubilant at the news. "Mama will be so excited Miss Lucy. I can't wait to tell her," said Sampson, after giving them directions to the house.

Lucy was so excited she could hardly sleep. She and Emma rose at five the next morning, wanting to get an early start. Lucy had never been more than thirty miles from where she was born. She marveled at everything she saw. Emma could not help but laugh and tease her mother. They were having a marvelous time. Around noon, Emma mentioned she was getting hungry. Lucy pulled out a sack of snacks she had packed that morning. Emma laughed at the sight. "Oh Mama, we will be eating in a restaurant for lunch today. You've hardly eaten anything the last two days and I want you to have a good meal before we get to Coretta's."

"But Emma, I've never eaten in one of those fancy eating places before," said Lucy, wearily.

"A Kentucky Fired Chicken place is hardly a fancy restaurant, Mama. We will get us some fried chicken and mashed potatoes with gravy, just the way you like it," said Emma, as she pulled the car into the restaurant parking lot. It suddenly hit her that her mother had never eaten in a restaurant before. She felt a surge of sadness for her mother and wondered why they had not paid more attention to her. She vowed that would not be the case any longer. Now that Junior was gone, there would be no reason she couldn't visit her mother and take her places any time she wanted.

Lucy reluctantly got out of the car and followed Emma inside. She sat shyly while waiting for their food and was amazed at how fast it was ready. She had never tasted chicken so good in her life. She forgot about her shyness and enjoyed every morsel. They finished their meal, used the restroom and got back on the road. They would reach Coretta's within a few hours.

Lucy sat quietly now, worrying about how Coretta would feel about what she had to tell her. She will probably hate me, she thought. I could have told someone what I knew and her husband might still be alive. She was beginning to feel a little sick at her stomach. Emma noticed her mother had gotten quiet, and suspected the reason.

"Mama, you know Coretta won't blame you for what happened to Earl. It was all the result of a bunch of evil men, Daddy among them," said Emma quietly. "She was your friend and I am sure she knew of your predicament with Daddy. You are doing the right thing Mama, and I am sure Coretta and her children will appreciate what it has cost you to do so."

"Oh Emma, I hope so. I do hope so," Lucy sighed.

Coretta and her youngest son lived in a small house on the outskirts of the city. Emma told Lucy it was called the suburbs. Lucy had never seen so many houses in close proximity to each other. They were all about the same size with little difference except for the colors. There were white houses, blue houses, yellow and grey. Some had shutters, some had porches, but most impressive to Lucy, was the neatly trimmed lawns and the flowers. Coretta's house was yellow with brown shutters. Yellow mums bloomed along the base of the house. Lucy was so happy that Coretta had done well after moving away.

Emma and Lucy had just stepped out of the car when Sampson and Henry came dashing out of the house.

"Miss Lucy, you don't know how good it is to see you. And is this Miss Emma?" asked Sampson, not sure if he was correct.

"Yes it is Sampson, and please, call me Emma. No more of this Miss Emma business. Makes me feel old," said Emma, with a laugh.

"And this is little Henry, I assume," said Lucy, reaching for Henry's outstretched hand.

"Yes Maam, only I'm not so little anymore," said Henry. "Can I get your bags?" Mama woke up early this morning and has been ordering us around all day. Clean this, move that. We haven't seen her this excited and alert in weeks."

"Thank you so much for coming Miss Lucy," said Sampson, reaching for Lucy's bag. Lucy hoped she would have use for it. After hearing what Lucy had to tell her, Coretta might order her and Emma out of the house.

Emma and Lucy followed the two young men inside. "You all have a seat and make yourselves comfortable while I fetch Mama," said Sampson. "She spends most of her time in bed now but she instructed me to fetch her as soon as you arrived."

"Oh Sampson, we can visit in her bedroom if she would be more comfortable there," said Lucy, shocked that her friend was so enabled.

"No, Miss Lucy, she gave us strict orders. I'll be back shortly. Henry, fetch the ladies something cool to drink while I get Mama," Sampson said, as he left the room.

Lucy sat twisting her hands in her lap. Emma could see she was an emotional wreck but knew she could do nothing to relieve her mother's anxiety. Only a few moments had passed when Lucy looked up to see Coretta being helped through the door by Sampson. She was so frail and thin, Lucy hardly recognized her.

"Lucy girl, you're a sight for these old eyes," said Coretta, reaching for Lucy's outstretched hands. "I couldn't believe it when Sampson told me you were coming to visit. They stood looking at each other for a moment, then hugged each other tightly as tears started to flow. They had both been through so much but the bond was still there.

"Let's get you into your recliner Mama," said Sampson, gently leading his mother to the chair. "Henry and I will excuse ourselves and start dinner while you ladies visit."

"I'll come help you boys," said Emma, rising from her seat. She knew it would be easier for her mother to tell Coretta the purpose of her visit if it were just the two of them.

"Well tell me, how have you been Lucy? Sampson told me about your house and I was so happy for you. I know how I felt when we moved in here. I must have laid in that tub an hour the first time I took a bath," Coretta laughed. "I still marvel at all the modern conveniences and I never take a thing for granted," she finished, sounding a little out of breath.

"It does take some getting used to. The first week I was there, I would find myself heading outside for the outhouse every time I got the urge to pee," said Lucy, and both women broke into giggles.

"I don't want to tire you out Coretta. Sampson told us about your illness and I want you to know how sorry I am," said Lucy. "I had to come see you when I heard. I know you don't know, but Junior died a couple of weeks ago."

"Lucy, I would say I am sorry for your loss, but to be honest with you, I never had much use for that man because of the way he treated you," Coretta said, hoping she didn't offend Lucy.

"I know Coretta. It's a terrible thing, not being able to grieve for a man you were married to for forty two years, but I can't. Junior was a terrible husband and an even worse father," Lucy said, and decided this was the opening she needed to tell Coertta, the main purpose of her visit.

"Coretta, I have something to tell you and you may order me out of your house when I do," said Lucy, taking a deep breath. I won't blame you if you hate me but I have to get this into the open for you and your boys."

"Whatever are you talking about Lucy? I would never do such a thing. You will always be welcome in my house," Coretta said, an uneasy feeling settling in the pit of her stomach.

"It's about Earl, Coretta," whispered Lucy, her head bowed. She could not stand to look her friend in the face when she told her of the awful thing she had done.

"Earl," said Coretta. It was still a very painful memory for her and just the mention of his name by Lucy brought all those feelings back.

"Yes. I should have done this long ago but at first I was terrified for my children. Then you and the boys moved away and the years slipped by," Lucy trailed off. She shook her head and took a deep breath. She had to finish this, get it done, once and for all.

"Coretta, that girl Earl was accused of killing, I knew all the time who did it." There, it was done. She had said the words, now she had to face what was coming.

Coretta looked at her as if she could not comprehend what she had been told. As the words sank in, Lucy could see the anger in her face and almost bolted for the door.

"You mean to tell me you knew Earl was innocent, yet you let those men chase him to his death," Coretta whispered.

"It all happened so quickly, Coretta. At first I didn't know for sure, but Junior admitted it to me later. The day that woman died, Junior came home with scratches all over him, burned his bloody clothes and warned me to lie for him if anyone came asking where he had been that day. I told him I would not lie for him, and for that, I took a beating. I was used to it but what really kept me quiet were his threats. He knew what meant the most to me and told me I would find one of "my little brats" dead if I didn't do as he said."

Coretta sat quietly, too stunned and angry to say a word.

Lucy continued, "You remember the night the Sheriff brought me over to stay with you when Earl died?" Coretta nodded. "When I got back home, I found my little Glory, only ten years old, lying in the floor with her thumb in her mouth, just like a baby. Junior was so afraid I was going to tell the Sheriff what I knew. He beat that little girl black and blue, just as a warning to me. I knew right then, I was trapped. As much as I wanted to tell, I felt I had to protect my children. Earl was already dead by then. I know you never doubted his innocence Coretta, but your boys deserve to know the truth. When Junior died, I vowed to make it right," Lucy finished, tears of relief and regret rolling down her face.

The two women sat quietly, tears rolling down their faces, neither looking at the other. It was Coretta who made the first move. After digesting what Lucy had told her, she knew she also would have done anything to protect her children. She could not blame Lucy for that. It would not have saved her Earl anyway. By the time Lucy knew for sure Junior was the killer, Earl was already dead. Coretta knew it must have taken a lot of courage for Lucy to bring this out into the open. She was so grateful that her boys would now know their father was not a murderer.

Coretta reached out her hand and patted Lucy's bowed head. "Lucy, I knew things were bad for you at home, but I never knew just how bad. I know this took courage and you will never know how grateful I am. You are right, I never doubted Earl's innocence, but the boys were young and didn't know their father as well as I did. I know there was that little doubt in their minds. I can go to my grave now, knowing my boys can have a good memory of their father, without that dark stain."

Relief swept over Lucy and every ounce of energy left her body. She slid to the floor, wrapped her arms around Coretta's waist and sobbed into her lap. Coretta gently rubbed the hair back from Lucy's face and softly whispered, "It's all right Lucy. It's all over now."

After dinner, everyone sat in the living room while Lucy and Coretta told the boys about their father. Coretta had asked the boys not to say anything until they were finished, for fear they would upset Lucy again. Henry did not seem to be affected by the news that much but Sampson was clearly shaken. Lucy could see the tears in his eyes and was sorry she had to bring this pain to them. She was relieved, however, when Sampson took her hand and said, "Miss Lucy, I know this wasn't easy for you. Henry here, he don't remember our Paw that much, but I do. I know Mama believed he was innocent but I just wasn't sure. Now I know, and I will forever be grateful for that."

They all slept well that night. Lucy could at last rest with her conscience clear and Coretta and her son's could rest knowing their father's name would be cleared. Lucy had explained to them how she had told the Sheriff and the records would be cleared as soon as she got back home.

Lucy knew she would never see Coretta again as she left the next day. The two women hugged each other and vowed to visit, each knowing it not to be true. Lucy received a call six weeks later from Sampson, telling her his mother had passed away. Emma took Lucy to the funeral where she said her last goodbyes.

CHAPTER 30

There was a lot of talk at first, as the news got out that Sara Mae's murder had been solved. As it turned out, most people were not surprised Junior was the guilty party. They held no animosity toward Lucy as most of them knew of the poor woman's plight. The men involved in Earl's death kept their heads low and their mouths shut.

Lucy worked for a few more years at the meat packing plant. She finally had to give it up as her health began to deteriorate. The children, or some of her grandchildren were a constant presence in her home. Lucy delighted in their visits and the grandchildren loved hearing Lucy's stories of her childhood. They would look at her in disbelief at some of the stories she told them. They found them hard to believe but knew their Grandmother would never lie. Lucy's sisters, Greta and Marcy came to visit quite often now. They felt bad about staying away before but could not stand to see the way Junior treated her. Though in poor health, Lucy was happier and more content than she had ever been.

Lucy went quietly in her sleep one night, which was the way she wanted. No nursing home, no burden to anyone. That was her plea to God every night. To the end, she was still thinking of others. The church was filled to over flowing at her funeral. Lucy would have been shocked at the affection and admiration so many felt for her. She was laid to rest next to her mother on a bright sunny day. At last, Lucy McGregor was home and at peace.